Charlie
is a
CHICKEN

JANE DENITZ SMITH

Charlie is a CHICKEN

HarperCollins*Publishers*

Charlie Is a Chicken
 Printed in the United States of America. For information address HarperCollins Children's Books, a division of HarperCollins Publishers, 10 East 53rd Street, New York, NY 10022.

Library of Congress Cataloging-in-Publication Data
Smith, Jane Denitz.
Charlie is a chicken / Jane Denitz Smith.
p. cm.
Summary: When she falls under the influence of the boy-hating, snobbish Jessica, fourth grader Maddie is manipulated into turning on her best friend Charlie and joins Jessica in sending him spiteful anonymous notes in school.
ISBN 0-06-027594-4
[1. Friendship—Fiction. 2. Schools—Fiction.] I. Title.
PZ7.S6497Ch 1998 98-20000
[Fic]—dc21 CIP
AC

1 2 3 4 5 6 7 8 9 10

❖

First Edition

Visit us on the World Wide Web!
http://www.harperchildrens.com

For Henry the First

"It's easy. All you have to do is pull yourself up, one foot at a time," Maddie explained, reaching overhead. "Pretend the branches are steps." She climbed higher and higher into the pine tree until all Charlie could see was one purple and one yellow sock.

Charlie cupped his hands together and hollered, "Okay, Maddie. I believe you. Come down."

Silence.

"PLEASE." He walked in a circle around the base of the tree and counted, "One-two-three-four, one-two-three-four," until she jumped in front of him and said, "Ta-da!" with her arms extended, like a circus gymnast who had just completed a tricky routine.

"Your turn." Maddie pushed Charlie toward the tree.

"I don't want to," he said.

Maddie stood with her hands on her hips. "You promised."

"Okay, okay," he said lightly, like he was giving in to something cinchy—like his mother nagging him to wear a sweater under his coat.

One foot, then the other, just like Maddie instructed. Charlie gripped the smooth, sturdy branches and continued to climb; a fan of needles tickled his face, but he didn't dare let go long enough to scratch. One foot after the other. It was easier than Charlie thought. He was eye level with his bedroom window now and so surefooted that he dangled one foot out into empty space.

And then everything changed. The limbs, so thick just a few steps earlier, bent with the weight of his body. He wrapped his arms around the top branch like a sailor clinging to the mast during a storm, and waited.

"Maddie," he croaked, his breath shallow and rapid. "MADDIE!"

And suddenly Maddie was there, one branch below him, with her hand tight around his ankle, telling him where to place his feet.

"You can do it, Charlie," she said. "You're almost there, Charlie," she encouraged him. "Here comes a bumpy branch. Put your foot a little more to the right. Trust me." She spoke to him every time he hesitated, and he listened to her until both feet touched the ground. His hands were sticky from pine pitch, and his legs felt all rubbery, like the first time he got out of bed after he had pneumonia last winter.

Charlie and Maddie looked up one more time into the web of branches, and then back to each other.

"Next time we'll climb up together," Maddie said. "I'll come from one side and you'll come from the other, and we'll see who the winner is." She grinned at Charlie and spread out her arms, spinning around and around.

Chapter One

The note crash-landed on Charlie's desk and Charlie figured it was from Maddie. Maddie passed notes to Charlie at least twice a day. Alison Burham, who sat between their desks, was so used to passing Maddie's notes to Charlie that all she had to do was clear her throat and he'd open his hand to receive it. The notes mostly had to do with after-school plans, but sometimes they just said, HI CHARLIE! with rainbows in all four corners.

But this note was different. It was purple and shaped like an airplane, and fell from the sky like a missile.

Luckily Mrs. Anderson didn't see. She had a pretty good sense of humor about most things—missing homework or chewing gum in class. But not note passing. Sometimes, when she intercepted one, she even read it out loud.

Charlie hid the note on his lap underneath his

desk. He could tell right away that it wasn't from Maddie. Maddie was left-handed, and when she wrote, her hand twisted like a claw, so the ink smeared across the page. This was written on pale purple notebook paper, but the handwriting was a fancy cursive. It could've been a letter his mother wrote, except for the wide-open circles over the *i*'s.

He flattened it out.

Charlie is a chicken.

Brilliant. It sounded like something a second-grade kid would say. Charlie looked up and tried to concentrate. "Footnotes," Mrs. Anderson said, and then something about "accurate sources," but after that all he could see was her mouth opening and closing like a marionette's.

Charlie is a chicken.

Maddie would laugh when he showed it to her. He turned around, but she was hunched so far over that her scraggly bangs brushed the top of the wooden desk.

Charlie is a chicken.

Charlie stared at the Daily Schedule.

8:45 Morning Meeting
9:00 Decimals
9:30 Library/Research
10:15 Recess
10:45 Reading Buddies

Charlie is a chicken. Charlie is a chicken. Like that stupid baby taunt. *Na-na na-na naaah-na.*

Maybe everybody knew about his note. Maybe it was a class conspiracy. He stretched his neck so he could see Thomas Mitkowski, who sat in the last seat of the last row. Sure enough, Thomas was looking right at Charlie. But all he did was smile, tug on his earlobes, and run his fingers through his crazy red, mad-scientist hair.

Charlie folded the note until it was small and hard as a superball and closed his fist tightly. "Time to head to the library," Mrs. Anderson said. "You'll need your research folders and a sharpened pencil. Line up *quietly,* please."

Charlie scanned the room for Maddie, but she was already standing behind Jessica McGuire, so he gathered his materials and walked by himself.

"Here!" Thomas called, and Charlie set his books down. Even though he liked Thomas, and sometimes had fun following his invention schemes, Charlie always avoided sitting next to him in school. Thomas talked so much that Charlie couldn't concentrate.

"Life Saver?" Before Charlie could shake his head no, Thomas stood up and reached into his pocket and pulled out a yellow one, fuzzy with lint.

"Thanks," Charlie said, examining it carefully and setting it down. "I'll be right back. I have to look something up."

The assignment was to write about a hobby they'd like to learn. It had taken Charlie a while to decide, but he finally settled on ventriloquism. He figured it'd be useful to know how to throw his voice, especially if his parents were calling and he was finishing an exciting chapter in his book. He could also surprise Maddie by making the Goodies talk without moving his lips.

Charlie walked to the research section at the other end of the library and sat on a little stool in front of the encyclopedias. He loved the library, with its books lined up in orderly rows and the tall metal shelves on either side that surrounded him like a secret fort. He heard voices, but he couldn't see anybody and nobody could see him.

He pulled out the V–Z volume. Venice. Violet. Volcano. Vulture. He set the encyclopedia gently on the floor and took out the crisp new pack of index cards his mother had bought for him.

He had just written down the Dewey decimal number in the left-hand corner when something sharp grazed his cheek.

Charlie sighed and waited. No other flying pieces of paper, no footsteps even. Only Mrs. Anderson's voice, calm and steady and far away, as if nothing had happened. Charlie looked at the paper airplane lying on the carpet, and his chest ached the way it did in gym class when Mrs. Nesbit made them run four hundred yards. There were no footsteps, but someone was there. He could feel a presence, substantial but invisible.

He bent down and slipped the airplane—this one was red—inside his notebook and moved across the library toward Mrs. Anderson. She was standing with her back to him, thumbing through the card catalog.

"Hello, Charlie," she said. "Are you finding everything you need?"

"I have to go."

She looked bewildered, so he tried again.

"I have to go to the bathroom."

"Of course," she said. She tilted her head in that worried way, and Charlie knew what was coming. "Do you feel all right, Charlie? Do you want to go to Mrs. Hammond's?" she asked, putting her hand on his forehead. "You look kind of pale."

Charlie wished he was sick enough to go to the school nurse's office. "I'm fine," he said. He smiled and walked down the long corridor of the school and around a corner to the bathroom. He opened the door to one of the tiled stalls, slid the bolt across, and took out the note.

Maybe this one was from Maddie. The first note might have been an accident, something meant for Travis Larson, whom everybody still called Screech Owl because he'd spent the first week of third grade screeching every time the teacher called on him. Or Abby Burlak, the girl in front of him with a million Girl Scout patches on her sash. Or Lucas Leonard, whose underwear showed out of the top of his baggy blue jeans.

Charlie studied the note again. *For Charlie,* it said in large, fancy cursive, clear as skywriting. He turned it over. It had to be him. He was the only Charlie in the fifth grade.

Charlie is a chicken.

Charlie took a deep breath and opened the new note.

Charlie smells.

The same fancy handwriting. A skull and crossbones in each corner of the paper, with little wavy lines all around.

Charlie smells. Charlie smells.

He read the note again. I DO NOT, he wanted to scream, so his words would bounce off the walls of the bathroom and out the door and down the halls and over the PA system from the microphone in the principal's office. Anybody who spent any time at all with Charlie knew that he didn't smell. He showered every night and flossed and brushed his teeth just as Dr. Hillman had showed him. In fact, he washed his hands before lunch and after recess, and even more during flu season.

Charlie smells.

He folded the note and put it in his pocket with the other one.

Maddie would know what to do. She'd get a handwriting sample of everybody in the class. Or she'd turn it into something fun. Maybe they'd be spies, like they were last summer, when they hid behind the yellow couch in Maddie's living room and tried to hear what her parents were getting her for her birthday.

Charlie double knotted his sneakers the way he always did when he was worried and walked back to the library. Maddie sat in the middle of the room sucking on the tip of her braid. He waved his hands to get her attention, and she looked up for a second. He was about to walk over and whisper that they had some important business to discuss, when he saw that she wasn't looking at him anymore. Her head was bent down, and she was giggling at something Jessica McGuire had said.

Jessica? Miss Perfect? Miss Popular? Miss Teacher's Pet? The girl they didn't even bother to ignore and only spoke to when they were forced to be partners. He waited, hoping Maddie'd look up again, but she didn't.

"What'd you do, fall in?" Thomas shouted. And then, as if that wasn't bad enough, he pressed his teeth together and made a whooshing noise that couldn't be mistaken for anything but the sound of a toilet being flushed.

"Boys. Please," said Mrs. Anderson.

Charlie's face burned—first his cheeks and then his ears and the back of his neck. He took one last look around to search for enemy signs and turned to his report.

Chapter Two

"You can be our partner too, Karen, if Mrs. Anderson says we're allowed to be in groups of three. But I did ask Maddie first." Jessica bent over the water fountain so that her shiny ponytail looped over her neck like a question mark, and then she stood back up and linked an arm through Maddie's. "Right, Maddie?"

Maddie's backpack slipped. The sharp claws of her lucky rabbit's feet that dangled off the zipper strap dug into her shoulder blade, but she didn't move. How could she, when Jessica—the very same Jessica McGuire who only yesterday aimed a dodge-ball straight at her stomach during gym class and didn't even apologize—had just chosen Maddie for her solar system partner? Only three weeks earlier, Jessica had brought birthday party invitations to school and had handed them out to practically everybody, but not to Maddie. And now, when Mrs.

Anderson told the class that half the solar system project would be graded on artwork, Jessica turned around and looked right at Maddie. She smiled so that all her teeth, straight and white as piano keys, showed. And she pretended she had to sharpen her pencil, but what she really wanted to do was give Maddie a purple lollipop with a tiny note taped to the top that said "Partners 4-ever."

Right after they broke into their groups, Jessica covered Maddie's ear so that everybody could tell she was whispering a secret. She told Maddie that she was a good artist—better even than Mrs. Mahoney, who had taught art at Lucy P. Haskins for at least a billion years.

"I'm a better writer than you are," Jessica said, "so I'll write the report. But you're responsible for the special effects. They have to be really big and really good. Okay?"

Maddie looked at Jessica and nodded her head. All Jessica had to do was ask, and Maddie knew she could never say no. She'd work all night on the solar system project and not even stop for supper. She'd hold the jump rope for hours during recess. She'd give Jessica the correct answers in the weekly spelling quiz—if she remembered them herself. She'd even steal a stick of Juicy Fruit gum from the top drawer of Mrs. Anderson's desk, where everybody knew she kept a secret supply.

And anyway, Charlie wouldn't mind. She looked

at him, bent over his desk and writing in his assignment book. He might even be relieved. Wasn't he always complaining about how disorganized she was, with her chicken-scratch handwriting? He'd probably end up writing the final draft, anyway.

Maddie turned her back to Jessica, but there was Karen Billings staring at her. Karen was new this year, and had always ignored her before.

"Hey, Jessica," she said, moving in front of Maddie, "can I have a Gummi worm?" She moved between Jessica and Maddie and stepped on the back of Jessica's white sneaker.

Jessica bent down and rubbed the black mark with her finger. "They're new, Karen. Thank you very much."

"Sorry," Karen said. "But can I have one?"

Jessica stuck her hand in her pocket and pulled out a blue worm. "Take it or leave it, as my father would say."

Karen snatched the worm. While she was chewing, she squinted at Maddie, and her narrow eyes shrank to almost a straight little pencil line.

"Anyway," Jessica continued, "we'll work on the project at my house. Nine planets shouldn't take that long."

Depends, Maddie thought. If you just want to make little blobby circles they'll take about five seconds, but. . . . Already Maddie's brain was racing. They could use clay, but they could also use other materials, like tinfoil. Maybe she could get two boxes at Rinehart's Electric, those huge ones that hold refrigerators, and they could stack one on top of the other. Then they could paint a black background, except it wouldn't be just black because nothing's only one color. It would be bluish-purplish black and there could be stars, and they could actually suspend the planets from the top of the tallest box with invisible thread. But—and this was the greatest part—instead of looking at the planets from the outside, you could step into the box so that you'd feel as though you were actually in outer space, floating in between Jupiter and Saturn.

Maddie turned to Jessica. "We can make an environment," she started to explain. "Like the one at the Science Museum. We can make it really fantastic—"

Maddie stopped. Her voice was doing it again—going up an octave and gulpy, the way it always got when she was worked up about something. And her arms were flailing in every direction, like the picture of the Hydra in her mythology book.

"You're the boss," Jessica said, and suddenly she slowed down to whisper something in Karen's ear—something that made them both laugh—and Maddie was left trailing behind.

Maddie rubbed the yellow rabbit's foot between her fingers. The yellow one was the oldest and most worn, but it was still her favorite. Then she lifted her backpack and followed. She knew Jessica would never wait for her to catch up, or look behind to make sure Maddie was still there. But it didn't matter.

Life was crazy, Maddie thought. One day you were as invisible as a broom in the broom closet, and the next day Jessica McGuire could be choosing you, out of everybody in the whole class, to be her partner.

"Maddie," Charlie said. He stood in front of her, blocking her path. Maddie set her backpack down between her feet.

"What?" Maddie asked.

"This won't take long. I have to show you something." Maddie watched as he reached into his pocket and pulled out two pieces of paper.

"Hurry, Charlie," Maddie said. "I have to go somewhere." But she knew it was useless; Charlie didn't know how to hurry.

Maddie put one hand on her hip, the way Jessica did, and sighed. Still Charlie didn't hurry. He opened the papers, which were full of creases, and placed them gently across his thigh and smoothed them with his open hand. He stood right in front of her, blocking her view, so she had to tilt to the side so that she could see.

Jessica was just about to turn around the corner. Maddie wanted to go, but Charlie spoke again.

"Look, Maddie," he said, and he pressed the papers into her hand. "Read them. Tell me what you think we should do."

"Not now, Charlie," Maddie said, handing them back without looking at them. "I'm going to be late." If she hurried, she could still catch up. She hoisted the backpack onto her shoulders.

"You need to clean that thing out, Maddie," Charlie said, shaking his head. "It's not good to carry so much weight. Besides, half of what you've got in there you could get rid of."

Charlie's words of advice hovered in the air like an irritating mosquito. "How do you know?" Maddie asked.

"I can guess," he said. "What you need is something like this." He shifted the canvas bag his mother had gotten him at the beginning of the year. It had separate compartments for each subject, and little slots so that Charlie's pens, pencils, and keys were perfectly arranged. Maddie couldn't believe that not too long ago she had asked her mother to buy her the same thing.

"I like my backpack," she said. She pulled down the sleeves of her sweater so that they covered her hands. "I have to go," she told him, and started down the hall. Jessica McGuire was gone, and it was all Charlie's fault.

"Don't forget," Charlie called after her.

"Forget what?" Maddie said.

"We have to fix the Goodie fort!"

Maddie turned around. The lunch bell rang and the hall quickly filled with people. Charlie was gone.

Chapter Three

Charlie waited for Maddie. Call *now,* he said to himself.

The wind rattled the glass around the old wooden window frame.

When I count to three, the phone will ring. One, two, *three.*

Silence. Just the tree outside scraping in the wind against the windowpane.

A gust of cold air blew, and Charlie pulled out the sneaker that held the window open a crack and it automatically slammed shut.

Yesterday it had been Charlie's turn to choose from the baseball cap the slip of paper that would decide their fate for the afternoon.

"Grass fort!"

"Distance-spitting contest!"

"Spy!"

"Food experiment!"

"Obstacle course!"

"Circus!"

They'd sat cross-legged on the braided rug in the middle of Charlie's floor while Charlie closed his eyes and lifted a piece of paper out of the hat and unfolded it.

"GOODIES," he yelled.

"I knew it," said Maddie.

Then they ran to the dormer window in the middle of the bedroom and kneeled down in front of the Goodies. The Goodies were the creatures Maddie had made out of a special white clay you could bake in the oven. They were no bigger than a pointer finger, with clothing carefully painted on. Maddie had been making them ever since kindergarten, and a boxful was under the bed—teachers, camp counselors, grandparents, kids from school. But ten of them always stayed on the windowsill. There were Charlie's mother and father; and Maddie's parents—whom she called by their first names, Paul and Josie; and Gideon, Maddie's baby brother; and Maddie's pets: Pokey, the turtle; Poppy Eyes, the goldfish; and Freckles, her dog, who was hit by a car three years ago.

"Let's make the Gideon Goodie be in charge. He's got to drive the car to the supermarket and make supper. It's going to be ice-cream sundaes with rainbow sprinkles," Maddie said.

But that was yesterday. Today Charlie sat alone.

He wiped a speck of dust off the top of the Charlie Goodie's head. Come on, Maddie, he thought. Maybe she was on her way. Maybe she was riding her bike down the street with her helmet tilted at a crazy angle because she never took the time to put it on right.

He positioned the Goodie so that it faced the glass, and looked down to the pavement below. The Goodies lived at Charlie's; he and Maddie both agreed that that was the best place for them, because Maddie's house was messy.

Charlie's house was always tidy, with books that didn't tumble out of their shelves, and dishes from a week ago that were neatly put away, instead of stacked precariously in the dish rack.

Besides, Charlie had a great bedroom. He used to sleep in a room next to his parents', with a bunk bed and a long shelf across one wall where his collection of model ships was displayed. But Charlie always wanted to move to the attic. He remembered, even when he was little, climbing the steep, narrow stairs and sitting on the old armchair with the yellow filling that spilled out. Even though he hated to climb high—he avoided ladders and even the monkey bars at the playground—Charlie loved the way the world looked so peaceful and orderly from up above.

When he first suggested changing rooms, his parents reacted as though he was asking if he could move to across the ocean. They found a million crazy reasons to say no. It was too drafty, especially in the winter. Where would they store all the furniture that was up there? Most of all, they worried that they wouldn't be able to hear him if he called in the middle of the night. But Charlie said they could put a trail of night-lights in the downstairs hallway, leading up the attic stairs to his room, and they finally gave in. Maddie loved it and called it her second home.

Charlie held the Goodie in the palm of his hand. Maddie had given Charlie that first Goodie a long time ago, when she'd come to his house for a sleepover. She had gently peeled off the plastic wrap and made Charlie close his eyes tight as she laid it in the palm of his hand. "It's for you," she said, and Charlie had answered, "Goody," and that's how the Goodies got their name. The Charlie Goodie had a nose that tilted upward, like Charlie's did, and big feet, too. After the Charlie Goodie came the Maddie Goodie with bangs and long braids. Year after year, the Goodies collection grew until Charlie's windowsill was covered with them.

Charlie placed a Kleenex pillow under the Maddie Goodie's head. Suddenly there was a loud rap on the door, followed by a series of soft, rapid knocks.

"Finally," Charlie said, and he jumped off his bed and ran downstairs. "I wondered when you'd get here." He opened the door, but instead of Maddie, there was Thomas Mitkowski, with his hair standing straight up and glistening under the light in the hallway.

"So, Charlie, here's my plan," Thomas began. "Today we're going to make a water system."

"A what?"

"A water system. Every city needs a water supply. Hence"—he pulled out a long, clear tube from his safari vest—"this essential piece of equipment, compliments of my aquarium. Do you have any wire?" Thomas was always searching for supplies—wire, string, bottle caps, rubber bands.

"I don't think so," Charlie replied. Just the thought of looking for wire, not to mention building a water system, made Charlie feel tired.

"That's no problem. Besides, we'll make cement from the mud, and when it bakes in the sun, it'll hold. Plus"—he pulled a huge wad of gum from his mouth—"we can use this if we have to," he said, and he popped the gum back in. "Hey, what are these?"

Thomas touched everything when he came over. Sometimes Charlie wished he could figure out a warning system, so he could take his special things off the shelves and hide them in a safe spot before Thomas arrived.

"What?" Charlie stood behind him. Thomas was holding the Thomas Goodie by its neck.

"This looks like me," Thomas said.

"Of course it does. It's a Goodie. You've seen them before."

"But not this one. He's got green boots. Just like mine. And his hair—" Now Thomas was dangling the Goodie from its wrists.

"Don't!" Charlie snatched the Goodie from Thomas and returned it to the windowsill.

"But we can use these," Thomas said. "They can be the work crew."

"No, Thomas." Charlie grabbed his jacket, and Thomas followed. When they were halfway down the stairs, the telephone rang and Charlie stood still. Maybe it was Maddie calling . . . but no, he could hear his mother talking to his aunt about some tag sale the next weekend.

Charlie sighed. "Let's go," he said.

They first stopped at Charlie's father's gardening shed, where they found a watering can and also a spade, and then they ran down to the edge of the creek. The current was so strong that dead leaves from the willow tree rushed downstream. Charlie was tempted to take his sneakers off and dangle his feet in the running water. But then a cloud covered the sun and he shivered.

Thomas crouched and dug a long, narrow tunnel. Charlie watched as he carefully placed the tube inside and covered it with dirt, so that only transparent little tips poked through. "Assistant Engineer," he ordered, "engage the water supply."

"What?"

"Fill the watering can. Hurry! Come on!" Thomas

yelled. "There's a drought. All the cows are keeling over!"

Charlie dipped the can in the stream. Then he ran over to Thomas.

"Disengage!" Thomas screamed, and Charlie crouched down and emptied the watering can's contents next to the tube where Thomas pointed.

Nothing happened. The water lay in little puddles on top of the rocky soil.

Charlie walked to the other side. Suddenly, water shot through the opposite side of the tube with such force that it squirted Charlie in the face.

"Again!" Thomas directed. His arms were flailing and his hair was wild. "They need more water! More!"

Charlie kept pouring water while Thomas screamed. Charlie was careful to stay away from the other end of the tube.

"And now," Thomas announced, "we need to make a trap for a water shrew."

"Why?" asked Charlie.

"Because this trap is different. When the shrew steps on this little piece of wood"—he grabbed a twig from the embankment—"it'll release a pulley, made out of a string with a rock suspended on the end, and a piece of Limburger cheese will descend." He dug into his pocket and produced a long strand of gray string.

"I'm kind of tired, Thomas," Charlie said.

"I'll do all the construction. You can be my apprentice."

"No, thanks." Thomas looked disappointed. "Maybe tomorrow."

"Maybe," Thomas replied. "If I'm not working on my viaduct."

They climbed the bank of the creek together and lay on their backs. Charlie looked up at the sky. The clouds were moving quickly, and, far away, the trees nearest the top of the mountains were no longer bright with autumn color. Charlie got dizzy watching—as though he was a cloud, skimming across the sky. Maybe he was looking down at his house, at the school, at Maddie. She would wave to him. "Send me a string and pull me up too," she'd call. Maybe they'd have a spitting contest on their cloud, to see who could spit the farthest.

A loud, razzing sound broke the silence.

Thomas was sitting up, blowing hard on a thick blade of grass. He paused long enough to grin at Charlie, gulp, and release a low, long belch that picked up force, like lava cascading over the side of a volcano. Then he gave a satisfied sigh, as if he'd just finished a twelve-course meal, and lay on his back again.

Chapter Four

"Other hand," Jessica ordered, and Maddie obliged, splaying her right hand across the top of her fractions notebook. Jessica dipped the nail polish brush back into the triangular bottle and withdrew it, wiping off the excess polish on the side. In front of her on the school playground, Maddie could see a game of Don't Touch the Gravel, and for a second she wondered what Charlie was doing. She'd never called yesterday. Maybe he'd decided to work on the Goodie fort without her.

Persian Dawn was the name on the bottle, and that's just how Maddie imagined the sky in Persia would look when the sun came up from behind a mountain: It would glow softly, a combination of gold and pink and orange. She glanced at the other bottles lined up on steps to the playground. Heartbreak Red. Sinful Fuchsia. Fireball. Maddie liked all of them. But Persian Dawn was her favorite.

"You have to stop biting your nails," Jessica told her. "Otherwise it won't look nice."

Jessica wound a loose thread on the bottom of her faded T-shirt around her pinky and yanked. Her blue jeans had a perfectly round hole at the knee, as if she had cut it out with a scissors. And if Maddie had been wearing that T-shirt, her mother probably would have told her to escort it directly to the rag pile in the laundry room. But on Jessica it stayed magically tucked in, and the frayed threads were as evenly spaced as the fringes on her mother's silk shawl.

Maddie squinted and looked at Jessica, using her artist's eye—the one her father told her to use when they visited the museum. By itself, nothing about Jessica was that special. Her nose was kind of on the longish side, if you were completely honest. One front tooth overlapped the other a little bit, and her feet, with their seashell-pink toenails, were actually wide. Jessica was a lot like the Impressionist paintings Maddie loved: Up close they weren't much more than a jumble of dashes and dots, but stand back even a tiny bit, and they came into perfect focus.

"Ewww," said Karen, waving her bright-red fingernails in the air to dry the polish. "She really does chew them."

"I'm trying to stop," Maddie said. "I don't even know when I'm doing it. I think it's when I'm reading. I get really distracted—"

"It's a disgusting habit," Jessica interrupted. "My

mother said you can get sick putting your fingers in your mouth."

I will never put my fingers in my mouth again, Maddie vowed silently. She had never noticed her nails before, but now that she looked at them—all jagged and even a little bloody from where she gnawed the cuticles—she was embarrassed, like the time in first grade when she hung upside down on the monkey bars and her underwear showed. Never again, she repeated to herself. Wasn't there some bitter-tasting polish that you could buy that would remind you to cut it out every time your nails crept up to your mouth?

"My mother knew somebody who died because they bit their nails," Karen said, and even Jessica looked like she didn't believe her.

"Come on, Karen," Jessica said, rolling her eyes.

"She did," Karen insisted. "She never washed her hands, not even after she used public restrooms, and she got the flu and died. That's what my mother said."

Liar, Maddie said, but not out loud. Liar, liar, pants on fire. As she waved her right hand in the air and Jessica gently applied polish to the left, Maddie studied Karen. Her cheeks were round and puffy as a marshmallow. There was a little patch of flesh from her elbow to her wrist that puckered when she yanked up her turtleneck's sleeves. If I stuck my finger in there, I bet it would leave a mark, Maddie thought. Or maybe it would just close around itself, like when she poked her finger into the yeast bread her mother was always making.

"You know what's really funny, Maddie?" Jessica asked.

"What?" Maddie ran her tongue over her shiny fingertips.

"Well, before I knew you, like two years ago, I used to think you were a boy."

Maddie remembered. People always used to mistake her for a boy, and she actually took it as a compliment. It wasn't just because the only time she wore a dress was on picture-taking day. It was her hair, too. Her mother called it a pixie cut, but in fact, her hair was more like a crew cut; she loved the way the short little ends at the back of her neck felt.

"I'm growing it out now," Maddie said. "See?" She stretched her bangs in front of her face. "My bangs are almost as long as the rest of my hair."

"But you have to get rid of the split ends," Jessica said, gingerly touching a tip of Maddie's hair. "It'll grow faster if you do."

"Okay," Maddie said.

The first recess bell rang, and Jessica scooped up the bottles of polish like they were jacks. She put them in a little flowered bag and put that bag inside her backpack. "Time to go," she said, and Maddie stood up and followed.

From behind, Maddie studied Jessica's hair. It was

soft as velvet. She watched as Jessica pulled her blue gingham scrunchie out in one movement that was as smooth as a magician untangling an intricate knot. Then she wound it over and over again until her ponytail was perfectly in place. Maddie was so busy watching that she didn't even notice Charlie standing next to her.

"We played Capture the Flag," he said. "I looked for you."

"Sorry. I was busy," Maddie said.

"Doing what?" Charlie asked.

"Stuff."

"I gave Maddie a manicure," said Jessica, and she turned around. "See?" She grabbed Maddie's hand and held it toward him.

Charlie looked at Maddie. "Why?"

"Why not?" said Maddie. She looked at Jessica, who smiled. Maddie's voice gained strength. "I think it looks nice."

"So do I," Jessica added.

"Okay," he agreed, but he didn't sound convinced.

Jessica put her arm around Maddie's shoulder. "It's not like she needs permission or anything."

Maddie dug her heel into the gravel.

"Want to come over after school?" he asked.

She shrugged her shoulders and looked at Jessica.

"Maybe," Maddie whispered.

"What?" Charlie asked.

"I said *maybe*, Charlie."

"Because I have something to show you."

"Okay, Charlie."

"Why are you whispering, Maddie?" he asked, but before she could think of an answer, the doors to the school opened.

"Wait, Maddie," said Jessica, before they walked into Mrs. Anderson's classroom. "I want to tell you something. Something PRIVATE." She looked at Karen and waited for her to walk away. Then she whispered: "You can be my second-best friend." Maddie felt a flutter in her stomach. "But there's only one rule."

Even before Jessica said a word, Maddie knew she'd do it. Maddie would do anything Jessica wanted.

"It's about boys. You can't be friends with boys." Jessica lifted the garnet birthstone that hung from a chain around her neck and pressed it between her lips. Then, carefully controlling the water fountain, she bent over and neatly took a drink.

Maddie took a drink after her, but she turned the handle too hard, and the water sprayed in her face.

Chapter Five

"Did your mother tell you?" Charlie asked as he watched Maddie peer inside the pumpkin on Charlie's kitchen table and then reach into it and pull out a handful of stringy orange pulp.

"Tell me what?"

"Heather Hills."

Maddie tore off a paper towel and wiped her hands. "Heather Hills," she repeated. "So?"

"Our parents said we're old enough to go this year. Finally! We're free! We can go trick-or-treating at Heather Hills all by ourselves."

"Alone?" Maddie asked. "To Heather Hills?"

Heather Hills was the only apartment complex in town. It was less than a mile away, but with its pool, tennis courts, golf course, and man-made ponds in front of each brick building, it felt like it was practically in another country.

"Think of all the candy!" Charlie shouted. "I'm

bringing a pillowcase, just to be safe. Thirty apartments times five buildings! That equals a lot of candy. We'll have candy until Valentine's Day."

"I don't know," Maddie said. She stabbed the pumpkin with the knife and begin cutting with the serrated edge.

"What?" Charlie studied her face. She didn't even look excited.

"I might be busy, Charlie," Maddie said. Charlie heard their parents' voices coming from the living room, soft at first, and then erupting in laughter. Charlie guessed his father was telling one of his political jokes again—the ones he had to ask him to explain.

Maddie wiped her hands on a paper towel and continued carving the pumpkin's features: thin, arched eyebrows first, then two nostrils that faced each other like half-moons.

"The mouth is the hardest part," she explained, "because if you don't concentrate, the teeth get pointy, like a vampire's. And now I shall make yet another incision—" She let out a giggle as she continued cutting. "Remember the time I let you carve the nose and it ended up as big as a cantaloupe?"

"Come on, Maddie." Charlie stood up and pushed his stool closer to the table, so his knees were pressed against its edge. There'd never been a trick-or-treat without Maddie. It was a tradition, like candles on birthday cake or turkey on Thanksgiving.

"Charlie, didn't I just say this is the hardest part? I have to concentrate," Maddie said sternly. He looked at her, surprised, but she was smiling.

"I think I'm going to give this guy another face, on the other side." Maddie continued cutting as easily and accurately as if she was using scissors. It was incredible. Maddie would forget to close her backpack, so her paper and pencils always fell out. She wore clothes that didn't match on purpose, like one purple sock and one red. She never remembered to do her homework until Charlie reminded her. But somehow she could carve a pumpkin as skillfully as if she was performing brain surgery.

"There. What do you think?" She turned the pumpkin around. One side had a wide, screaming mouth. The other side had a clown smile.

"A masterpiece, as usual, Maddie." He sipped his soda before continuing. "Well?"

"Charlie, it's not that big a deal." Maddie flicked a slimy pumpkin seed and it landed on the edge of the sink. "Don't get so excited."

"You have to go. It's a rule."

"You're the one who likes rules. Not me. I'm surprised you don't think it's dangerous to go to Heather Hills. You're such a chicken, you don't even cross School Street without getting off your bike."

A chicken? Charlie's head was suddenly stuffy, like someone had turned the heat up too high.

Charlie is a chicken.

"That's not true," he said. "Why are you saying that?"

Maddie looked up and smiled. "Take it easy, Charlie. I'm just teasing you. Besides," she said, "aren't we getting a little old for trick-or-treating?" He couldn't see her face because her bangs were hanging down.

Suddenly Charlie's father appeared. "Who wants hot mulled cider?" he asked, as everybody followed—Charlie's mother, holding a tray of crackers and cheese, and Maddie's parents, and Gideon, who was about to plunge his fist into a bowl of onion dip.

A cold drizzle was falling by the time Charlie and Thomas got to Building A. They sat down in the lobby to warm up and compare trick-or-treat bags. Also, Thomas needed to adjust his costume, which kept climbing above his waist. It didn't matter that not one person could identify what he was. First they'd look at Charlie, who was a mummy. "Wow, that's a lot of old sheets," more than one person had said, as they admired the strips of cloth wound tightly around his entire body so that only his eyes, nose, and mouth showed through. Then they'd look at Thomas, who was supposed to be a gyroscope. A hula hoop covered with gauze formed the base of his costume, but the rope that held it up kept slipping off his shoulders. Everybody said it was "interesting" and "creative," but no one ever guessed.

"Did you get any of these?" Thomas pulled a tiny wax milk bottle out of his bag. He bit the lid and a little of the green syrup trickled down his chin. Then he popped the entire candy into his mouth and chewed vigorously.

"You can have mine," Charlie said. He hated milk bottles. The wax tasted dusty, and the syrup was as thick and sweet as cold medicine.

"Thanks."

Charlie and Thomas cased the entire building, walked outside, and sat on the wet curb, watching as other trick-or-treaters walked down the street, sometimes in pairs but mostly in groups. Once in a while the drizzle would stop and the moon would come out between the clouds. Voices swirled all around, like leaves that flew in the chilly night air.

Three trick-or-treaters came toward them with their arms linked. The tallest one, the one in the evening gown and high heels, wearing a tiara and holding a gold wand, was in the middle. Charlie could make out a pirate on one side, and on the other a kind of halfhearted black cat with black sweatpants, black turtleneck, tail, and a mask that sat on the top of her head.

"Hi Charlie," the princess said, and Charlie looked up. It was Jessica McGuire. She tapped him on the head with her wand. "What are you?" she asked Thomas. "A nuclear disaster?" But she turned away before he had a chance to answer. Charlie recognized the new girl, Karen. And then he turned to the cat, who was now standing a few feet away, leaning against a light pole.

"Maddie," he said.

Maddie pulled her mask over her eyes and scraped the road with the heel of her black ballet slipper.

"You told me you weren't going trick-or-treating. You said—"

Maddie shrugged her shoulders and reached inside her pillowcase for a miniature bag of candy corn.

"You said you might be busy," Charlie continued. "That's what you told me."

Jessica smiled and her bright-red lips spread wide, but it was a creepy smile—like a witch's, Charlie thought, and he flinched as if she was about to pinch him. "Maybe she didn't want to go with *you* . . ." Jessica answered, as she stood next to Maddie and put an arm protectively around her shoulders.

"Why didn't you tell me you changed your mind?" Charlie whispered, but Maddie only shrugged her shoulders again, and wouldn't look him in the eye.

"Are you stupid?" Jessica sputtered. "She *didn't* change her mind. She just didn't want to go with you." Then, noticing Thomas, she said, "And what are you staring at?"

"You," Thomas said. "Your evil powers will never penetrate this megawatt flesh."

Jessica rolled her eyes and readjusted her tiara, which had tilted to one side. Then she tapped her wand, first on top of Charlie's head and then Thomas's. "Be gone, I order you!" she said, and like an ocean liner she sailed down the street.

Charlie waited. Sure enough, Maddie looked at him, but as soon as their eyes met, she turned away.

Chapter Six

Maddie was writing a list. THINGS TO TALK TO JESSICA MCGUIRE ABOUT. She lay on her stomach and gnawed on her pencil, thinking. She propped Buster Bear against the headboard of her bed, so that they were face-to-face.

"You're a mess," she told him. "Your stuffing is coming out, you lost another eyeball, and you smell." She pressed his fuzzy stomach against her nose and breathed deeply. He did smell, a combination of maple syrup and bubble bath, dust balls, and chocolate.

"Now listen to my ideas," she said as she leaned on her elbows. "Mrs. Anderson. Gym. Nail polish. Pets. Beads? Do you think she likes beads?"

Jessica had called to invite Maddie to go ice-skating at the public rink downtown. "It's from eleven to one, and it costs two fifty," she had said, "unless you want some extra money for hot chocolate."

"I'll ask Josie," Maddie had told her.

And Jessica had giggled. "It's so weird how you call your parents by their first names. I could never do that."

"Sounds good to me," Josie had said. She seemed happy that Maddie had a new friend, and even offered to give her her allowance early, in case she wanted to buy something for herself on the way home.

Only two hours to go. An hour and a half, if you counted the time it would take to walk there. That's why she needed to make a list. What if Jessica didn't have anything to say? What would they talk about? Books? TV shows? It was important to be prepared.

"Maddie," Josie called, "I need you to watch Gideon!"

Maddie sighed and kicked the cover off. She climbed out of bed and searched for the cleanest pair of sweatpants she could find lying on the floor.

Jessica was already waiting on the long wooden bleacher by the time Maddie arrived. She was wearing black leggings and a rainbow-striped sweater, and each skate had a pink pom-pom on the toe.

"I'm not very good," she said. "I used to take lessons, but I'm out of practice."

"Me too," Maddie lied, and she pulled off her boots and put on her skates. They were hockey skates and they had belonged to her father when he was a little boy. After years of waiting, Maddie was finally big enough to inherit them. Even though they were worn, the leather was soft and supple, and when she wore them, she flew, backward and forward, around the rink.

She yanked the laces and one snapped.

"Great," Jessica said. "Now what are you going to do?"

Maddie licked one frayed tip of the loose lace and double knotted it onto the other. "I'm ready," she said, and she stood up.

"Aren't those boy's skates?" Jessica asked, looking down at Maddie's feet.

Maddie looked down too. Before she could think of an answer, Jessica shouted, "Come on!" and held out a white, furry mitten that looked like a paw. Maddie grabbed it. They skated around twice and then Maddie let go. She bent her knees and put one hand behind her back like a speed skater and whooshed around the rink. Organ music played, but she hardly heard it. She wiped her nose on her sleeve and noted, as she whizzed past, parents pulling up little kids who had fallen down and an unsteady girl tiptoeing across the ice while she held on to someone's hand. The air smelled thin and metallic, and she pulled the sleeves of her turtleneck over her hands to keep them warm.

"Maddie! Maddie!" Jessica called her from the center of the rink, but Maddie was going too fast to stop, so she went around one more time. Then she came to a neat stop, spraying ice behind her.

"Watch this!" Jessica said, and she tilted her head back a little bit, held her arms out like a ballerina's, and made a few careful rotations before stopping. "I studied ballet, so it's not that hard."

Maddie nodded in agreement. She had studied ballet too, but that was years ago, when she was in kindergarten. She liked the spinning and jumping, but could never follow the teacher's steps.

"Need some?" Jessica pulled open a tube of lip gloss that hung from a string around her neck and rubbed it over her mouth.

"Sure," Maddie said, and held out her hand.

"Smell it. It's guava. I also have tangerine, strawberry, and kiwi."

"Where'd you get it?" Maddie asked.

"The cosmetics aisle at the supermarket," Jessica said. "It also comes in lip-gloss pots."

Maddie made a mental note to go with Josie the next time she drove to Stop 'n' Save. Josie hardly wore any makeup at all, except for moisturizer and mascara, if it was a special occasion. She'd probably laugh at Maddie when Maddie told her what she wanted.

"Thanks," Maddie said, and handed it back.

"Anytime, Maddie." Jessica linked her arm with Maddie's, and they skated in perfect rhythm over to the wall.

"So—" Jessica began. "What do you think of Scott Myers?"

Maddie rubbed her red hands together and put them up to her cheeks. Last year, in addition to Charlie, of course, she'd actually invited Scott Myers to her birthday party, not to mention Elliot Edwards and Thomas Mitkowski, too. They went candlepin bowling, and her mother made a cake that looked like a rainbow. What should she say?

"Well?" Jessica asked, and Maddie was pretty sure she knew the right answer.

"He's disgusting?" she tried.

"I know," Jessica agreed and Maddie nodded with relief. "He has germs. And he tries to give them to me at recess. I hate boys. Don't you?" Jessica wrapped her powder-blue scarf around her neck. She tilted her black beret to one side, and Maddie noticed that her pink ears were small and translucent, like seashells.

"I don't like boys," Maddie said quickly. "Except for my brother, of course. He doesn't count, right?"

"Of course not," Jessica said. "Karen doesn't like boys either. And you know who we don't like most of all?"

"Who?" Maddie studied Jessica's face, calm as always.

"Charlie Siegel."

Maddie imagined herself spinning so fast in the middle of the skating rink that she was just a blur and nobody, not even Jessica, could recognize her.

"Karen says he likes you."

"He does not," said Maddie. She could see Karen now, with her tight little pigtails and her squinty little eyes, and that squawky laugh Charlie said resembled a bird in the rain forest.

"She says he wants to marry you."

"Yeah. Right." It wouldn't even occur to Charlie to say something so dumb.

"He thinks he's so great," Jessica continued. "He thinks he knows everything. What do *you* think of Charlie?"

"Me?" Maddie paused for a second that seemed to stretch on forever.

"I can't stand him," she heard herself say. "Really and truly," she added, for emphasis. Then she tilted her head to one side the way Jessica did, like she was listening to music far away.

"Karen and I are having a sleepover." Jessica slid her hand across her blade and removed some snow. "It's only for girls who don't like boys. Karen and me and maybe you."

"I don't like boys," Maddie said again. If she said it enough, maybe it would be true.

"Good. You are now officially my second-best friend, and you are officially invited to my sleepover." Jessica slipped her arm around Maddie's, and they skated hand in hand around the rink.

Chapter Seven

"If you put ketchup on the bun like this"—Thomas demonstrated, pushing his chair closer to the table—"and mix it with a little mustard, it looks exactly like gangrene."

Charlie bit into his celery stick with cream cheese.

"And now"—Thomas turned two french fries into enemy soldiers. Then he poured chocolate milk onto his plate—"a snake-infested jungle." In plopped the french-fry soldiers.

"Food is not a toy, Mr. Mitkowski," the cafeteria monitor warned.

"I'm planning to eat it." Thomas popped the soggy french fry into his mouth and grinned at the monitor, then turned to Charlie. "Want to come over after school? I have a new gerbil." Thomas always had some new animal. So far the list included tropical fish, a hamster, a box turtle, and a cockatiel.

"I thought you already had a gerbil," Charlie said.

"That one died. This is a new one. She's very social. Wait'll you see what I'm making her. It's a trampoline. It's got little springs under a handkerchief. Can you come?"

"I don't know," said Charlie. "I might be busy." Even though he usually ended up having fun, Charlie always had to be convinced before he'd agree to go to Thomas's. Maybe it was because Thomas's bedroom was messy and smelled funny—a combination of cloudy fish-tank water and cedar shavings. Maddie's room was cluttered too, with clay and markers and clothing spilling out of her dresser drawers, but he liked being there, sitting on her enormous striped pillow, or watching her dip her brush into her watercolors and make a couple of squiggles and lines turn into a real picture. He wondered if she had finished the most recent Goodie. It was going to be Mrs. Anderson, complete with her black shirt and the long silk scarf she liked to wear around her neck.

Suddenly, the playground monitor blew her whistle and the entire fifth grade stood and ran toward the doors that led to the playground. Thomas pushed ahead to finish the tunnel he had started under the tire swing, and Charlie followed.

Charlie dug his hands deep into his pockets. He had to talk to Maddie. But all through recess she stayed close to Jessica and Karen. She looked different, he thought with surprise. He could see her eyes because her bangs were pulled back by a new barrette shaped like a sunflower, and she was wearing a lip-gloss necklace that dangled in front of her coat.

After the bell rang, Charlie went to his locker to hang up his coat. When he walked to his desk he saw it: the third note. It sat in a white envelope like a party invitation, but he knew what it was.

Don't look front.
Don't look back.
You are stupid.
That's a fact.

Charlie tried to laugh. Back and fact don't even rhyme, you moron, he almost said out loud. He hoped whoever wrote the note was watching as he stood up and made a point of opening the lid to his desk and dangling it by one corner, as if it was a dead rat, before letting go.

At afternoon recess he was determined to tell Maddie about the notes. He walked toward her, blowing little rings with his breath.

Maddie held one end of a long jump rope and Jessica held the other. They swung the rope in wide arcs and it clicked against the blacktop. Karen swayed back and forth several times before she rushed in.

"Maddie?" Charlie tapped her on the shoulder.

"What, Charlie?" she said as she continued to turn the rope.

"I wanted to ask you something."

"Well?" she said. "I'm listening."

"It's important."

Maddie looked up, and in an instant the rope slapped against Karen's leg and she tripped over it, falling flat on her knees.

"Way to go, Charlie," Karen said.

"Sorry." He was surprised that she even knew his name. "Maddie, it's important."

Maddie set her end of the rope down on the ground and turned to him. "Can't you see I'm busy?" she said.

"Yes, Charlie," Jessica added. "Why don't you go bother somebody else?" She gathered the jump rope like a lasso around her elbow, and Charlie walked away.

Chapter Eight

Maddie sat on her bed staring at her "Math Facts" worksheet. She was invited to Jessica's house on Saturday to work on their solar system project. That was three days away. Two if you didn't count today, which was practically over anyway, since it was almost time for dinner.

She looked at down at the jumble of numbers that didn't even begin to make sense. It didn't help that she could hear her mother singing one of her show tunes at the top of her lungs.

Shut up! Maddie thought as she slammed her door.

She wondered if Jessica's house was also a loony bin. Not likely, she thought. Her family probably sat down to a quiet dinner every night, with classical music in the background. They probably played board games after dinner, Maddie thought. The last time she had pulled out a board game—it was

Monopoly—Gideon had grabbed a handful of real estate and dumped it in the toilet.

She also wondered if Jessica hated math as much as she did. The fifth grade was converting fractions to decimals, and she still didn't know how to subtract. "Borrow from the next column," Charlie always reminded her, and Maddie would nod her head and pretend she understood, even though she didn't. Borrow? You borrow sugar or a pencil. But numbers?

Maddie took a deep breath and looked down. The first column was easy and she was hopeful, but then she was lost. She made her eyes stay wide open until they started to tear, and when they did, she looked down at the numbers again. This time they were fuzzy and didn't look like numbers at all—more like hieroglyphics or old-fashioned wallpaper. Maddie took her pencil and started to decorate the numbers, putting spirals and curlicues on the tips of them, and sun rays around each of the zeros. Then she remembered that Mrs. Anderson was going to collect this worksheet and she tried to erase, but the outlines of her designs still showed through and the paper ripped.

"Maddie! Paul's home!" Josie called, and Maddie hopped off the bed and hurried downstairs. Every Wednesday was take-out night, and they always ordered the same thing: wonton soup, sesame noodles, orange chicken, and shrimp with vegetables. The candles were always lit, too, even in summer when it stayed light until long after dinner was over.

Gideon sat in his high chair, next to Maddie. He grabbed a fistful of sesame noodles and shoved them into his mouth.

"Bon appétit," Josie said, lifting her wineglass.

"Gross, Gideon!" Maddie said.

She watched her parents pluck food from the cartons with their chopsticks and wondered if she should try to use them again. The last time, the food was practically gone by the time she was able to get some into her mouth, and Josie had to make her a peanut butter and jelly sandwich instead.

"So how was your day, my favorite daughter?" Paul asked.

Maddie answered the way she always did: "I'm your *only* daughter."

"Really?" he teased. "I thought I had another daughter, hiding under the table." He bent over and pretended to look.

"Nope. I'm your only daughter." Maddie rolled her eyes, and he laughed. She loved the little crinkles like tissue paper that gathered at the corners of his eyes whenever he smiled.

"Tell me everything you learned in school today." Paul pushed his wire-frame glasses down to the tip of his nose.

"We studied maps. We're starting a unit on Japan."

"Hmmm," he said.

"Cut it out, Gideon!" Maddie yelled. Gideon was

pulling on her sweatshirt, and his hand was covered with grease.

"Japan. And why Japan?" Her father taught English at the community college, and whenever he asked her about school, she felt like she was one of his students. She tried to think of a good answer, an answer that would make him smile at her and say "That's my girl," but all she could think of was "Different cultures?"

"Are you asking me or telling me?" Paul wanted to know as he reached for the rice.

"Different cultures," she repeated. "Last year it was Native Americans. This year is the Far East."

"Hmmm," he said, but she could tell he had already lost interest.

"Jessica McGuire wants me to come over on Saturday," she said. "We're doing a solar system project."

"And who is Jessica McGuire?" Paul looked at Josie.

"You remember the McGuires," Josie said. "He's a lawyer. I don't know what she does."

"I didn't know you two were pals," Paul said, peering over the top of his glasses.

"Kind of." Maddie looked at Gideon, who was smearing duck sauce all over his face. "He's disgusting. I'm going to throw up."

Josie plucked a shrimp with her chopsticks and said, "Be a little charitable, please."

Suddenly there was a muffled ring. Josie stood

up and uncovered the phone, which was buried under a pile of old *National Geographic* magazines.

"Maddie," she said, "it's for you."

"Hi, Maddie," Charlie said.

Maddie sighed. Life would be so easy if she could take Charlie and Jessica, and her parents and Gideon too, while she was at it, and arrange them wherever she wanted them to be, kind of like the Goodies.

"Charlie," she said. "Hi. What do you want?" Maddie waited. Charlie was so quiet on the other end of the line that she wondered if he was still there. "Charlie?"

"Do you need help with your math?" he asked finally. "I can show you how to do it if you want. You know, those problems are easier than they look."

"I think I get it," she lied.

"Are you sure? Don't forget to put the decimals in the right colums."

"I know, Charlie." She looked at Josie and Paul laughing. Like this was a normal dinner and nothing had changed. "Charlie—" There was something she wanted to say, but the words wouldn't take shape. She must have been speaking softly, because Charlie didn't seem to hear.

"Sorry about recess," he said. "Karen tripping and everything."

"That's all right. It doesn't matter." And it didn't. Not now, at this moment. Funny how it had made her so mad just a couple of hours ago.

"I'm doing my Writing Response Journal," Charlie continued. "I'm writing a story about a ball that talks."

Maddie looked around, as if Jessica was hiding in a corner of the living room. Then she wrapped the cord around her waist and settled on the floor. "Is it funny?" she asked.

"Yeah. It's pretty funny. There's all these adventures. This piece of bark carries him down a river."

"Maddie!" Josie called. "Tell Charlie you're finishing dinner. You'll call him back later."

"Josie says I have to go, Charlie. We're still eating. It's Chinese night. It's disgusting."

"I'll tell you more about it tomorrow, then," Charlie said, as if tomorrow was going to be just another plain old school day.

"Okay, Charlie." Now that she was talking to him, Maddie wished she didn't have to hang up. On the phone everything was normal. And there was something she wished she could tell Charlie, something he'd know how to fix. What she wished she could tell him about was this:

In the multipurpose room, just before Assembly started, Jessica had whispered, "I have a present. As long as you stay away from Charlie Siegel." Then she pressed a friendship bracelet made out of blue and purple embroidery thread into Maddie's hand. "Now you have to give me something too."

"But I don't have anything," Maddie had said.

"It can be little. It doesn't matter." So Maddie had

dug deep into the bottom of her backpack until her fingers reached the bottom. She could feel old crumbs and wads of paper, but suddenly her hand cupped around something cool and hard. She pulled it out. It was a pebble, small as a dime but perfectly round. Charlie had given it to her on the first day of school and told her it was a good luck charm. She had to rub it every time she got nervous before a big test. Before Maddie had a chance to change her mind, Jessica had snatched it. "This'll do," she had said. "Now our friendship is sealed. Read this. This is our present for Charlie. What do you think?" Jessica handed Maddie a slip of lined paper just as the lights dimmed and the movie about Mexican holidays began. Maddie had to hold it in her lap and wait.

"Maddie!" Josie called out again.

"Maddie," Charlie said, "are you there?"

"I'm here. I have to go, Charlie. Josie's getting mad."

"Okay. See you."

"'Bye, Charlie." Maddie slowly hung up the phone.

If I were a dog
And you were a flower
I'd lift up my leg
And give you a shower.

"What is it?" Maddie had asked as soon as the

lights were turned back on.

"I told you," Jessica answered. "We don't like boys. We write them notes, only they don't know the notes are from us. It's fun."

Maddie read the note again. "Why Charlie?" she wished she could ask, but she didn't.

"Really good," she had answered instead.

"That's what I thought," Jessica had said, and she fingered the friendship bracelet on Maddie's wrist. "It's your turn to write the next one," she had said, and Maddie had heard herself reply, "With pleasure."

"Maddie!" This time it was Paul's voice, and she came back to the table and sat down. But her rice was cold and she wasn't hungry anymore.

"Nice of you to join us," Paul said. "Who was that?"

"Charlie," Maddie answered.

"Who else?" Josie added, winking.

Chapter Nine

Charlie came downstairs in his pajamas to say good night. He knew his parents wouldn't bother asking if he had brushed his teeth and finished his homework because Charlie never needed to be reminded.

His father sat in his tweed armchair—the one Charlie's mother bought for his father's bad back—and read the newspaper. His mother read her mystery novel. Charlie looked at the clock on the mantelpiece. It was nine o'clock.

He walked over to each of them and kissed their cheeks. "Good night. Sleep tight. Don't let the bedbugs bite," his mother called after him as he walked toward the stairs.

I will now look into my crystal ball and predict the future, Charlie thought. In half an hour my father will stand up and stretch and say, "Another day, another dollar." My mother will also stand and check the locks on the front and back doors, and make sure the porch light is off. They will brush their teeth and then the faucet will stop, and the hall light will be turned off. One or both of them will come upstairs and make sure I'm asleep. I will turn over so they don't see my eyelids twitch, and I will also lie on top of the covers so they can't pull the blanket over me.

Charlie folded the bedspread at the end of his bed and lay on top of his sheets. If he didn't crawl under, he wouldn't have to worry about making his bed in the morning. It was another rule, like the others. Sleep on top of sheets. Wear clean socks and underwear to bed. Wake up before the alarm clock rings. Double lace sneakers. Put milk money in the right pocket of pants. Line pencils up according to size, like Papa, Mama, and Baby Bear. Sometimes all his rules made him feel cozy, like the old baby quilt he still slept with. But other times they just made him tired, and he wished he could set them loose in the air like soap bubbles.

The digital clock on Charlie's night table clicked on the quarter hour. A car radio thumped a couple of blocks over. Except for his toes, which he wiggled in his socks, he lay still, listening to the click of the baseboard heater. If he waited a little longer, until after his parents checked on him one last time and went to bed, he could actually hear the floorboards groan and shift, as if they, too, were turning over and going to sleep.

This is the quietest house I know, he thought. Sometimes he felt like the silence was his fault. He tried to be noisy. He dribbled the basketball his mother had given him even though he didn't like basketball. Or he watched Saturday-morning cartoons with the volume turned up, even though most of them were pretty stupid.

It was best of all when Maddie came over. Then the house was cozier and more spacious at the same time. She actually had her own special stool next to the counter, where she'd sit and talk about nothing important—Mrs. Anderson's new haircut or her favorite painting in the museum. She liked to watch his mother while she was cooking dinner. Once she was helping cut carrots for a salad and one of them flew in the air and landed on Charlie's head. She laughed so hard that Charlie and his mother started laughing too, until their stomachs hurt. Suppers with Maddie were like a party. Charlie remembered the place cards they used to make and put on everybody's plate so they'd know where to sit. Milk was knocked over and splattered across the floor, but it was wiped up without any comment. The table was filled with more food, and everybody had seconds. The overhead light seemed brighter than usual, and voices overlapped until they weren't four voices but one.

But as soon as Maddie left, the house was quiet again, almost as if it, too, was disappointed. Charlie and his father would dry the dishes and put them away, and they'd set the table for breakfast, with three clean placemats and napkins and spoons for cereal.

Charlie lay on his back with his eyes open. It wasn't that he minded not having a brother or a sister. But it did make him tired sometimes, being the only one.

Chapter Ten

"Hurry up!" Maddie urged her mother. Josie was sitting next to Gideon, feeding him bananas or apricots or something that looked a lot like throw-up. "I'm going to be late."

"You're going to get overheated if you don't take your coat off," Josie said, calmly pushing another spoonful into Gideon's mouth.

"I'm always late for everything," Maddie said. "Jessica's waiting for me."

"Did I tell you Charlie called again?" Josie asked.

"Yes." Maddie sat cross-legged on the floor and retied her white sneakers with the sparkly laces. They weren't exactly like Jessica's—hers were purple—but they were close.

"How is Charlie?"

"He's okay, I guess."

"Because I miss him," Josie continued. "I never see him anymore."

Maddie looked up. "He's dripping," she said.

"What?" Josie looked at Maddie, and then back at Gideon. The baby looked as if he'd grown a tiny golden beard.

"Is Charlie all right?" Josie asked, wiping Gideon's face with a damp paper towel.

"How am I supposed to know?" Every time Maddie turned around, it seemed some grown-up was asking her about Charlie. First thing yesterday, just after Morning Meeting, when everybody else was working on their current events reports, Mrs. Anderson called Maddie to her desk.

"I'm worried," she said. Maddie hoped she wasn't about to tell her something personal about her feelings, the way Josie sometimes did. "It's about you and Charlie."

Maddie acted confused.

"You used to be such good friends, and now—" She waited a few seconds to see if Maddie would complete the sentence, and then continued, "you both seem to be keeping your distance."

"It's nothing," Maddie said. She glanced longingly at her desk, wondering when Mrs. Anderson would release her.

"Because I'm good at helping kids work things out." She looked hopeful for a second and then smiled in resignation. "That's what I'm here for."

"Maddie—" Josie said.

Maddie looked at her mother.

"Is Charlie all right?"

"Why is everybody always so worried about Charlie?" Maddie stood up and slammed a chair against the table so hard that Gideon jumped.

Josie steered the car into Jessica's circular driveway and leaned over to kiss Maddie's cheek. Maddie walked up the curving brick path to the front door and stood between two tall columns carrying a long stick and a brown paper bag filled with solar system supplies. Next to the shiny black door was a wrought-iron bench painted red. The door knocker was shiny brass with the face of a lion. Maddie ran her fingers over it and wondered if she was supposed to use it, or if it was just a decoration. She looked down at her clothes. Even though she had laid them out with care the night before, she knew now that they were all wrong. The cuffs of her sweatshirt were frayed, and the sparkly laces only made her sneakers look dirtier than they already were.

She sighed and pressed the doorbell with her forefinger. From somewhere deep inside the house, four chimes sounded. Maddie waited and waited and wondered if she had the day wrong. And then the door slowly opened.

"Hello," said Jessica. She dipped a spoon into a glass bowl of vanilla pudding. "Wipe your feet."

"Hello," said Maddie. She looked down at the doormat and noticed that Jessica was wearing fuzzy green slippers with poppy frog eyes. She wiped her feet and stepped into the black-and-white-tiled foyer.

The ceiling was miles away. A chandelier as big as a spaceship hovered over her head dripping with crystal. A white table with gold edges held two vases in a smoky green glass, and in between was a clear bowl filled with pale-pink seashells.

Out of the corner of her eye Maddie could see a room that looked like a library. It had a leather couch, bookshelves, and an enormous desk. Every flower, every shell, every book on every shelf seemed to belong exactly where it was.

How could she ever invite Jessica to her house? The first thing that greeted you as you walked into the mudroom was a smelly box of Kitty Litter, plastic bags filled with bottles for recycling, and a tower of old, yellow newspapers that hadn't been removed in months.

"Come on. I'll show you my room," Jessica said. Her slippers rustled across the hardwood floor.

"Okay." Maddie's voice boomed, like it was blasting through a megaphone.

She followed Jessica up one set of stairs and through a living room with a shiny white piano, and they stopped in front of a sliding glass door. Jessica released the lock and the door slid open with a whispery sound. Maddie looked ahead, first at a brick patio with a wrought-iron table and chairs and then, beyond, to an oval swimming pool.

"That's pretty," Maddie said.

"My mother says it's more maintenance than it's worth," Jessica replied, and slid the door shut with the same soft *shhhhh.*

Maddie followed Jessica through a shiny white kitchen, down a hallway, and up a flight of stairs. The wood floor had given way to rose-colored carpeting that was soft and deep. Maddie wished she could take off her shoes and dig her toes into it.

"We have to be quiet," Jessica whispered, pointing to a closed door. "My mother's taking a nap."

"Oh," said Maddie. "Is she sick?"

"Of course not. Lots of people take naps during the day."

Good luck trying to nap in my house, Maddie thought. She could walk into a room and nobody would even notice—Paul was too busy pounding his fist on the kitchen table making a point about the news, or her mother was on the floor wrestling Gideon into a pair of snap-up pants. She usually escaped to her room not to nap, but to get away from all the commotion. Once she had recorded the hours until somebody bothered to call upstairs for her. Three. Three hours until they even noticed she was gone.

Jessica opened the door to her room, and Maddie stepped inside. There, sitting at a yellow desk, was Karen, sorting through a box of beads.

"Karen's here," Jessica announced.

"Hi," Karen said, without looking up.

Maddie turned around. There was a high bed that you'd have to stand on your tiptoes to climb into, with a lacy canopy over the top. A window seat was covered with pink-and-white gingham cushions and stuffed animals—just bears, from what Maddie could see. That's where I'd sit, she thought. I'd curl up there and draw pictures in my notebook.

"I'll give you a tour," Jessica offered.

"Okay," said Maddie.

"These are my books. And this is my horse collection"—she pointed to a glass case filled with ceramic horses—"and this is my dollhouse, even though I don't play with it anymore, and this is my desk"—she plopped down for a second on a white wicker chair—"and these are my board games and this is my jewelry box and these"—she held up a red basket painted with flowers—"are my hair ornaments and this is my closet. You can walk in it."

Jessica opened the door to her closet. Sneakers and loafers and velvet party shoes with little heels rested in their own little hanging pockets. Dresses and blouses hung from wooden hangers, and there were clear boxes with sweaters arranged from yellow to red to purple to blue. Maddie ran her finger across the length of the clothes.

"So. We better get started," Jessica said. Maddie stood back as she pushed against the closet handle and the doors glided together.

"What's in that bag?" Karen asked.

She stood next to Jessica as Maddie kneeled down and dumped the contents of the paper bag on the floor.

"They're balls," Jessica said, as a lime-green tennis ball disappeared under the scalloped ruffle of her bedspread.

"They're balls now," Maddie said, scooping them together. "But in a little while they're going to be nine planets." Jessica frowned, but Maddie kept talking. She had thought this through the night before and knew exactly how it was going to work.

"See," she said, holding up the largest ball in the pile, "this is our sun, and the nine planets"—she held up a Ping-Pong ball, a squash ball, a jacks ball, a round pink rubber ball—"will be revolving around this sun." She looked up. Karen looked doubtful, but Jessica was definitely interested.

"How do you get them to stick?" she asked.

"Simple." Maddie reached for the long stick—it was actually the handle of an old broom—and stood up. "Thumbtacks. String. We attach the string to the handle, and voilà! A three-dimensional solar system."

"Wow," said Jessica.

"So I'll work on this while you write the report."

"I already wrote it." She walked over to her desk and held up a couple of neatly typed pages. "I'll just watch you." She sat on her bed and opened a purple plastic box. Then she cut three strands of embroidery thread—orange, black, and yellow—and safety-pinned them to the coverlet.

"What are you making?" Maddie asked.

"Friendship bracelets."

Maddie watched as Jessica looped one strand over another and then pulled tightly. Then she looked at the friendship bracelet on her wrist. "Are they hard to make?" she asked.

"Not really. I have tons of them." Jessica pulled out a fistful of bracelets and dropped them on the bed. "I already gave you one, so this one's for Karen." She handed the other girl a thick bracelet with a slanted pattern.

Maddie looked down and continued working. Attaching the balls was easy. She pressed the thumbtacks into the balls with her thumb, and wound some string around each flat silver circle and then to the broom handle, making sure to space them evenly, so they didn't knock together. She held it up and readjusted Saturn.

Next came the hard part—making the solar system come alive, so that when you looked at it, you really felt like you were high above Earth, floating in empty, endless space. Maddie reached into the paper bag and pulled out strands of cellophane she'd saved. They were silver and gold, but best of all, there were a few deep-blue strands. She taped the cellophane to the handle so that it hung down and overlapped. Finally, she took out her gold marker, the one that went on like shimmery paint, and she tapped the cellophane over and over again.

"What's that supposed to be?" Karen asked, pointing to the blue streaks.

"A meteor shower," Maddie said.

"A blue meteor shower?" Karen looked at Jessica and giggled.

"I like the way it looks," Maddie said. She held the pole away from her, and the planets swayed against the shimmery strands.

"I do too," Jessica said, "but remember what Mrs. Anderson said. We're being graded on creativity and accuracy. If you take off that blue stuff, we'll definitely get an A."

One by one Maddie yanked the blue strands, and they fell in spirals to the floor. Jessica was right. It was a silly idea. Nobody would be able to tell they were supposed to be meteor showers.

"Now that that's done," Jessica said, snapping her friendship bracelet box shut, "you have one more thing to do."

Maddie looked at her blankly. She didn't understand.

"Your note to Charlie. Remember?"

Chapter Eleven

Maddie sat on her bed and chewed her pencil.

Watch out, she wrote and then crossed it out. It sounded too much like traffic directions.

Watch your step. That sounded sort of spooky. The only problem was, Charlie always watched his step. If somebody was sending a note to her, *Watch your step* might have made sense, but not to Charlie. She pulled hard on the tip of her hair so it reached the corner of her mouth and sucked on the bristly little tip.

Go fly a kite. She'd heard someone say that once. *Go fly a kite.* Knowing Charlie, he'd do exactly that. He would know just how fast to run to get it up in the air, and then he'd probably take the string away from her because she wasn't doing it the right way.

She made little grooves in the yellow pencil with her thumbnail and tried to imagine what it would be like to be Jessica, with a pink bedroom and a mother who slept most of the afternoon and—and this was the part Maddie still couldn't get over—who gave her permission to take a carton of butterscotch ripple ice cream out of the freezer an hour before supper.

When Maddie had needed to go to the bathroom, Jessica had pointed down a long, carpeted hallway that passed in front of a bedroom with the biggest bed Maddie had ever seen. It had a mustard-colored satin headboard and a night table on either side, each with its own lamp. Were those dried flowers on the lampshades painted or real? Maddie had to touch. She looked around and walked in. They were painted flowers—daylilies with tiny black dots in the center. Maddie ran her finger over the little raised circle of paint. Then she sat on an edge of the smooth purple bedspread and bounced up and down. The pillows, which were long ovals, like dachshunds, jiggled, and one rolled against Maddie's thigh.

Maddie put it back where it belonged and surveyed a night table. It held a neat stack of thick, shiny magazines. The one on top had a picture of a blond woman on a horse, and in the background there was a mansion covered with ivy. Maddie sighed and looked up. On the other side of the room was a small table with a silver mirror lying facedown and shiny tubes of lipstick neatly arranged on a silver tray.

Josie hated makeup. She said it was like wearing a Halloween mask every day of the year.

Maddie touched the gleaming tubes as carefully as if they were arrowheads or shards of pottery in the Museum of Local History.

BOYS ARE BAD, GIRLS ARE GOOD, BOYS ARE BAD, GIRLS ARE GOOD, BOYS ARE BAD, GIRLS ARE GOOD. Wasn't that what Jessica told her? Maddie wrote it over and over in her notebook, first in big kindergarten block letters, then in cursive, then with flowery letters at the beginning of each word.

But why? she asked herself. Why BOYS ARE BAD, GIRLS ARE GOOD? Because, stupid. Just because.

She turned to a new page in the notebook and swiped her hand over its smooth surface. Suddenly there were voices—her parents' voices—and then they were yelling so loudly that even with the door to her bedroom shut tight, she could still hear them. Someone pounded a fist against the kitchen table and the walls rattled. Then they were whispering. And then there was laughter—belly laughs that were loud and deep. Maddie tiptoed to the edge of the stairs and saw Gideon with Josie's straw hat—the one with the silk baby's breath all around—on top of his head.

"Help!" Maddie said out loud. She imagined levitating over the rooftops and floating with her arms outstretched until she landed gently faceup on Jessica's mother's bed. "Maybe I was switched at birth, because I know I'm not part of this crazy family."

Maddie brushed her hair away from her face and pulled the two hard, spitty ends back. She joined them together with a rubber band and then found a red ribbon in her underwear drawer and tied it into a bow around the ponytail. There, now I can write, she thought. She smiled a little half smile and crossed her legs.

If I were a chicken
And you were a pheasant
I'd sit on your head
And leave a white present.

Maddie slammed her notebook shut and shook her head so her ponytail jiggled, and if you were looking from behind, you just might think Maddie Martin was Jessica McGuire.

Chapter Twelve

Charlie was sitting on the tire swing and studying the handwriting, the ink, even the paper the note was written on when Thomas Mitkowski tapped him on the shoulder and shouted, "Boo!"

"I know who wrote that," Thomas said.

"It doesn't matter." Charlie pretended to look at his watch.

"She did." Thomas pointed to Jessica, who twirled the metal chain of a swing tighter and tighter and then lifted her feet and spun until the chair yanked her back and forth and she stopped. "Last year Zachary Fisher was her first victim. She told him he was going to flunk because he was so stupid. Don't you remember that day he was excused from gym because he was crying?"

"I think I do."

"Then she picked on Mike Oppenheim, the third grader with one blue eye and one green eye in Mrs.

Frankel's class. Now I guess you're the lucky one."

"Lucky."

"Hey, check this out." Thomas reached into the pocket of his windbreaker and pulled out a matted blob. "Know what that is?"

"What?" Charlie asked, just as the playground whistle shrieked.

"Oscar's latest hair ball." The whistle blew again, and E.R.T. was standing on the steps with her hands on her hips, glaring.

E.R.T. stood for Evil Recess Teacher. Nobody knew her real name, and they all called her E.R.T. under their breath. She snatched their balls away whenever there was the littlest disagreement, and reported them to the principal if they were caught standing on the swings, and even when it was freezing outside she made them wait until they were completely silent and lined up straight.

Thomas was still talking when they arrived at the end of the line. Charlie stood ahead of him so E.R.T. could see that he wasn't the one who was being noisy.

Indoors, Charlie was a little queasy. It always took him a few minutes to get used to the succession of cold air and then warm, heated air pouring out of the radiators. He peeled off his scarf and then his coat. He sat down for a second and was about to put his head between his knees when he saw two purple rubber boots in front of him. He looked up.

There was Jessica, dangling his Writing Response Journal in front of his face.

"I thought you might be missing this," she said. She smiled nicely at him as if she was asking him if he wanted to play.

"Why would I be missing it?" he asked her. "It was right on my desk."

"Not exactly," Jessica said. "Why do you think I found it on the seesaw? Good thing you put your name on it." She dropped it into Charlie's lap and walked away.

Charlie looked down. The back cover was ripped, and on the front cover was the outline of a muddy boot. Charlie tried to wipe the mud off across his corduroy pants, but it only smeared. He held it across his chest and walked to his desk.

"Charlie," Mrs. Anderson said. Charlie looked up. "I hope you thanked Jessica for finding your journal."

"Thank you, Jessica," he muttered.

"You're welcome," she replied.

Chapter Thirteen

"Earth to Maddie." Maddie looked down at the script Jessica had written for the Thanksgiving assembly. "Try it again," Jessica instructed, "the way I told you to."

Maddie was a candle with a cardboard flame—the star of the holiday play, according to Jessica. But if that was the case, Maddie wondered, then why did Jessica, who was Princess Winter, have all the lines and get to wear a pink tulle dress that looked like Cinderella's, while Maddie had to put on a frizzy orange wig that made her scalp itch? It was no different last week, when they presented their solar system projects. All Maddie got to do was to hold up the planet mobile and point to each planet while Jessica read the report.

Maddie stood with her arms straight up.

"Stop blinking!" Jessica ordered. "Candles don't blink!"

At the other end of the room, Charlie was making a diorama about the hardships of the first winter in the New World. He was molding clay into food—tiny corncobs, mashed potatoes, cranberry sauce, and peas—and concentrating so much that his tongue stuck out of the corner of his mouth. Clay pilgrims sat end to end on a long cardboard bench.

That's my idea, Maddie wanted to yell. Those pilgrims are just like my Goodies. Only if I was helping you, they'd look better—not like snaky blobs with pencil pricks for eyeballs. I could even make a clay centerpiece with acorns. And the pilgrims' shoes should have buckles. You could use paper clips— She took a couple of steps toward Charlie to give him some advice when she heard Jessica's voice.

"Maddie!" she yelled. "Pay attention to your cues!"

Maddie turned back before Charlie even noticed.

Maddie curled in a corner of Jessica's window seat. It's more winter than fall now, she thought. She blew quickly, so her breath left circles on all six panes of the windows. M-A-D-D-I-E, she etched with her finger. Then she covered the tops of her feet with a chenille blanket and looked out the window. Only the other day a warm, soft wind had tickled her face and neck as she rode home from school. She had buried Gideon under a pile of leaves in the backyard and the leaves reminded her of a thick, richly patterned carpet.

But then, overnight, a storm brewed while she slept, and when she woke up, the branches of the trees were completely bare and the leaves on the ground were thick and black around the edges. And the wind had changed. The flag on the pole in front of school snapped angrily, like rolls of caps rubbed on the sidewalk with a stone. Maddie thought about the Goodie house they had made out of bark and moss under the pine tree. Had Charlie remembered to take it indoors?

"I watched him," Jessica said. "He took your last note and slid it inside his notebook and didn't even blink. He probably threw it away."

Maddie shook her head. "I bet he saves them," she said. "He saves everything. I bet he's got a special drawer for them in his desk at home."

"No he doesn't," Karen replied, even though she was looking at Jessica the whole time. "I saw him throw one in the garbage pail in the cafeteria."

"He did not," Maddie said.

"How do you know? I bet you're still his friend."

"Well?" Jessica turned to Maddie and placed her hands on her hips. "Karen asked you a question."

Suddenly Maddie felt like she was still in school, trying to decipher a word problem in arithmetic. She braided the fringe edge of the blanket. "I am not," she said.

Jessica walked toward Maddie and curled on the opposite end of the window seat. "See?" Jessica told

Karen. "Maddie says she's not."

Karen's eyes narrowed. "Then her notes have to be better. They're stupid. They're like letters to my grandma."

"You can make them better, can't you, Maddie? Turn around. I'll make you a bun." Maddie turned around and hunched her shoulders while Jessica's hairbrush glided through Maddie's hair.

"Why me?" Maddie asked. "Why am I the only one writing the notes?" It was easier to ask Jessica questions when she wasn't looking right in her face.

"Because you know him the best, Maddie," Jessica said. "We all have our jobs." Maddie could feel one of Jessica's hands hold the little cup of hair in place while the other wound a scrunchie over and over again until the bun was as tight as a lid.

"Jessica?" A tall, thin woman appeared in the doorway.

"Mom," Jessica said, and her voice turned soft and high as she ran and hugged her. Maddie noticed that the woman's dark-blond hair was pulled back tight with an elastic band, and not even one little strand was loose.

"Hi, darling," her mother said. She kissed Jessica's forehead. "Dinner's in fifteen minutes." Jessica hugged her again. "Sweetie, you're hurting me." She wriggled out of Jessica's grasp and readjusted her paisley scarf. "Hello, girls," she said. "I already know Karen, but who is this?"

"Maddie," Jessica said.

"Hello, Maddie."

Jessica stood on her toes and whispered to her mother, who looked at Karen and Maddie and then shook her head. "Not tonight, dear. I'm exhausted. Besides, I need a little more warning."

"Please?"

"No. And no whining. You know how I feel about whining. Now finish up." She left and closed the door behind her.

"Did you ask her if we could stay for dinner?" Karen asked.

"It's not a good night," Jessica answered.

"Maybe another time," Maddie said. "Or you can come over to my house for dinner. Josie really wants to meet you. She even said to ask you what your favorite food was, and she'd make it."

"Lasagna. And garlic bread."

"Me too!" Maddie said. "Whenever we have lasagna, Josie gets grape juice so I can pretend it's red wine." Maddie rolled her eyes. "She does stuff like that. Well? Can you come?"

Jessica stared at Maddie before she answered. "Maybe," she said, then added, "Probably not. I'm pretty busy most nights."

"Josie could call your mother," Maddie said. "They could figure it out."

"It's time for you to be picked up," Jessica said, and led Maddie and Karen to the phone.

Chapter Fourteen

After a big snowstorm that turned to rain, the roads were icy and Charlie put his bike away in the garage and walked to school. He didn't wait for Maddie anymore. One more rule to add to his list: Don't wait for Maddie or talk to Maddie or look at Maddie or sit next to Maddie in the lunchroom or be Maddie's partner on class field trips. Why bother? All she did was pretend he wasn't there, or, if she had to be next to him, sit as far away as she could, like he had cooties.

Just last week after school he had ridden his bike in front of her house. Her stuffed animals were lined up on the windowsill the way they always were, and the string of colored Christmas lights that outlined her window even in the middle of August were blazing. There was Josie in the kitchen, standing in front of the stove. And then the front door opened and she stepped onto the porch and hollered: "Hey stranger, get over here!"

Charlie leaned his bike against the curb and walked up the front path.

Josie was wearing a long print skirt with tiny bells that hung from its belt. They jingled when she hugged him and said, "The greatest kid in the universe has arrived!" Josie had been saying that to Charlie forever. He held his breath and waited until, sure enough, she kissed both his cheeks. "So?" she asked. "Are you going to come in or are you happy standing outside in the freezing cold?"

"I don't know," he told her. "It's kind of late."

Josie grabbed Charlie's hand and pulled him inside. She unzipped his coat like he was five years old again and led him into the kitchen. "I need your expert advice. Nobody around here tells me the truth." She held out a wooden spoon. "Taste this," she said. "Does it need anything?"

He took a bite from the tip. "A little pepper, I think." He peered into the bubbling pot. "What is it?"

"Vegetable stew. I had to do something with all that produce before it rots. You like it? Or are you still a meat-and-potatoes kind of guy?"

"Meat and potatoes," Charlie replied.

"Personally, I think it needs more salt, but that's just me," Josie said. And then, before Charlie could tell her not to, "Maddie! Charlie's on his way up!"

He opened the door to her room, but she was nowhere in sight. "Maddie?" he called.

"I'm down here," she said. "Under the bed."

He kneeled down and lifted her bedspread. "What are you doing?"

"Making a fort. Want to see?"

"I can't," he said, and sat on the bed and waited for her. "My dust allergies."

"Oh, right. I forgot." He waited for her to roll her eyeballs the way Jessica did, but instead she just smiled and said, "I have a surprise for you."

"You do?" He couldn't believe it.

"Look what I found." She opened the drawer to her desk and pulled out a plastic bag. It was full of balloons.

"Where did you get them?" Charlie asked.

"From the junk drawer in the kitchen. They're left over from Gideon's birthday. Here." She handed him a round yellow balloon and he tried to blow it up, but nothing happened.

"You have to stretch it first," she explained. "See? Like this." She took the balloon from him and pulled the neck wide. "Now try," she said.

This time Charlie's balloon inflated easily. He blew and blew until he thought it was sure to pop. Then he took it out of his mouth and tied the end.

One by one they blew up all the balloons until they covered the entire bed.

"They're parachutes," Charlie said. Thomas had showed him how to make them. He opened the desk drawer where Maddie used to keep rubber bands.

They were still there. So were her scented markers and the collection of funny pencil sharpeners. Nothing had changed.

Charlie tied a corner of a tissue to the tip of the balloon. Then he took off his shoes and stood on her bed. "One, two, THREE!" he said, and the balloon drifted to the floor.

Next they made parachutes for all the balloons, and put little plastic jungle animals—tigers, monkeys, hippos—on some of the ends to weigh them down. They stood on the bed, then the desk, then the bureau, which was the highest place of all, dropping their parachutes at exactly the same time to see whose reached the floor first.

"You know what we could do?" Maddie asked.

"What?"

"We could make *parachute Goodies.*" She hopped off the bed and reached under her desk for the cardboard box that held her clay. Charlie watched as she pinched together brown clay and then green until they became a rabbit and a grasshopper with two big red eyeballs. Even though the clay was still soft, Maddie was able to attach a tissue to the grasshopper's hind legs.

"Watch this." She held the grasshopper parachute in one hand, and with the other she dragged her desk chair over to the open closet door. She climbed on the seat of the chair and placed one foot on the inner doorknob, one on the outer, straddling the door. She reached high over her head so she could hold on to the top of the door.

"Move the chair, Charlie," she ordered.

"No, Maddie. You're crazy. It's too high."

She looked at him with the new look that he hated—the one that made him feel stupid.

"Charlie," she said, "just because you're afraid of heights, does that mean the whole world has to be afraid of heights too? Well? The chair?"

Charlie moved the chair and watched as Maddie gave a push against the wall and began to swing back and forth. Then she held her parachute high and let it go. The parachute glided to the floor just the way it was supposed to and landed on a piece of paper.

"Hand me yours," she ordered.

Charlie held out the rabbit and just then her foot slipped off the gold knob. One hand lost its hold on the top of the door and Charlie watched as her body twisted and she fell to the floor. At first she looked more surprised than hurt. She even managed to smile at him and say, "Well, that was brilliant."

"Everything okay up there?" Josie called.

"Yes, Josie!" Maddie said in a loud voice. But then she looked at Charlie and shook her head. Her eyes filled with tears, and the scrape on her shin, though not bleeding, was already turning black and blue.

"It hurts, Charlie," she whimpered, and he went to the bathroom off the hall and ran the cold water till it was as cold as it would get. Then he took a washcloth from the tub, ran it under water, squeezed it out, and carried it back to Maddie. "Don't," she said, hiding the bruise.

"Let go," he said, and he moved her hand and covered her shin with the cold washcloth. "Feel better?" he asked, and she nodded her head.

"Thanks, Charlie," she said, and smiled at him the way she used to even when they weren't alone.

Why are you being so nice to me now? he wanted to ask. Why won't you be nice to me tomorrow, in school? Maybe she'd have a reason that made sense. Then he'd show her his folder of notes and she'd laugh and tell him that whoever wrote notes like that must be a moron and that he should ignore them because the only thing that mattered was that she and Charlie were friends forever.

But Josie came upstairs to tell him that his mother was getting worried and it was time for him to head home before it got too dark. "You have to go," Maddie told him in the bossy new Maddie voice, and he hurried out the front door.

The next morning when he got to school, a new note was on his desk.

Charlie, Charlie, eyes of blue.
Charlie, Charlie, we hate you.
Go to sleep and never wake up.

Chapter Fifteen

Maddie set her alarm clock for six forty-five. That was the only way she knew she'd get up on time. Lately it seemed she could never fall asleep until right before it was time to wake up. She lay awake most of the night, her arms and legs stiff under the quilt like her old Miss Krissy doll. Even resting with her eyes closed she could feel the weight of Karen's irritated eyes. They were heavy as bowling balls pressing on Maddie's stomach. And there was Jessica, telling Maddie not to touch her things, even though Maddie had to touch—her sweaters, her scrunchies, even her pencils and schoolbooks. In Jessica's bedroom ordinary objects were transformed, as if King Midas lived there.

Maddie kicked off her quilt and set her feet on the cold wooden floor and reviewed everything she had to do in the next hour. Write the note. Get dressed. Eat Corn Pops. Kiss Josie. Kiss Paul. Kiss

Gideon if he wasn't covered with bananas. Leave the note in a strategic spot where Charlie would be sure to find it. Get to school before the final bell. By the time Morning Meeting began, Maddie would be as tired as if she had already been through a full day of school.

Maddie put her legs on the floor and sighed. It was still dark, and the windows were etched in icy patterns.

Maybe I could take a sick day, she thought. Sometimes Josie let her stay home. "Everybody needs a day off once in a while," Josie liked to say. But she knew she couldn't, because Jessica would be mad.

Maddie walked to her desk, where she kept her supply of cardboard from Paul's dry-cleaned shirts. She took out the black permanent marker she'd stolen from the kitchen—the one her mother didn't let her use because she'd once ruined a new tablecloth when the ink spread through to the other side of her paper—and pulled the cap off with her teeth. *You are fat*—she began, then quickly crossed that out. Charlie was so skinny that you could see blue veins under his skin. She thought of something else and began to write.

After she finished her lettering, she added alternating moons and stars around the border. Then she unraveled a long piece of plastic wrap—also compliments of the kitchen—and laid the cardboard on top and wrapped it neatly like it was a present. The plastic wrap was essential, especially in bad weather. She nested the sign carefully into her backpack along with a roll of masking tape and a box of thumbtacks and headed downstairs.

"Hello, early bird!" Paul called. He cleared a spot at the kitchen table.

"Hi," Maddie said, giving him a kiss.

"How about one of my famous soft-boiled eggs?" Paul asked.

Maddie shook her head.

"Come on, I'm not that bad a cook." Paul waved a pan in the air, but Maddie shook her head again.

"Then how about a ride to school today?" he asked, pointing to the window. The sky was getting lighter, but icy pelts pinged against the glass.

"No thank you," Maddie said slowly. It would be so cozy to sit next to him in the front seat with the heat on, listening to the classical music station that he always played in the morning.

"I miss my girl," he said as Josie walked in, carrying Gideon on her hip.

"What a night!" Josie declared. "This little monkey was up every two hours."

"Really?" asked Paul. "I didn't hear him."

"Yes, I noticed." Josie poured herself a cup of coffee. "Hello, Maddie." She walked over and ran her fingers through Maddie's hair.

"Ouch," said Maddie. "You're hurting me."

"How about a hairbrush?"

Maddie looked at the clock over the sink, the one she loved, that had steaming cups of coffee all around the circle where the numbers usually were. "I've got to go," she said.

"But you just got up," Josie said.

"I'm meeting Charlie," she lied. "We're doing a geography project."

"What kind of geography project?" Paul asked.

Maddie thought for a second. "Maps."

"Maps. Could you be more specific?" He got up to refill his coffee cup.

"I'm late, Paul. Charlie's waiting." She looked at the clock again and figured she'd have to run now if she was going to be absolutely sure Charlie wouldn't be ahead of her.

"Since when do fifth graders have to get to school half an hour early to do work? Isn't that pushing it?" Josie asked, handing Gideon a teething biscuit.

"It's extra credit," Maddie told her.

"I'd rather have you sleep a little later and not do the extra credit. You're starting to get circles under your eyes," Josie said.

"School's important," Maddie answered.

"That's debatable," Josie said as Maddie called "Bye." She slipped her boots on in the mudroom, grabbed her backpack, and ran out the door.

"You're not dressed warmly enough. It's snowing,"

Josie called after her, but Maddie pretended she didn't hear.

But it *was* cold outside. It was the kind of cold that made your eyes tear and your throat ache. Josie was right. She should have worn her scarf and hat. Mittens, too. But Maddie hated wearing extra clothes. They made her feel like she was suffocating. Besides, she knew, even when she was taking them off and shoving them into her locker, that she was sure to leave a mitten there at the end of the day, or lose her scarf on the jungle gym.

The sleet bit so hard into her cheeks that she felt like she was bleeding. Josie was always complaining that she looked pale, but now maybe her cheeks were as pink as Jessica's. Maddie unbuttoned the top of her coat and put her face—from her nose to her chin—deep inside and breathed that nice moist air that smelled like wet wool.

She walked with her head down, looking behind her to see the pattern her boots were making on the wet pavement. One block more and she could see the sledding hill. Some muddy brown grass poked through, but mostly it was slick with packed snow. Last winter Josie had sent Maddie and Charlie to the sledding hill with a thermos of hot chocolate and some popcorn that she had just microwaved, so when they opened a corner of the bag, steam escaped. Charlie always wanted Maddie to go sledding with him, but only if she steered. She tried to bribe him to tie his sled to hers and be the caboose, but he wouldn't because it was too dangerous. Typical Charlie.

Maddie tripped over a fallen branch. The tiny hole in the knee of her sweatpants opened, leaving a loose flap of material wide as her knee.

"Figures!" she said out loud. Go ahead, Charlie, she thought. Tell me I have to be more careful. The day was ruined before it started.

She stopped in front of a telephone pole just before the school parking lot and looked around. Some kids were coming, but she had at least a minute or two. She took the note out of her backpack, jabbed it with two thumbtacks—one on the top and one on the bottom, just to be safe—and stood back to see how it looked.

Cold air rushed through the opening in Maddie's pants. Then her nose started to prickle. CUT IT OUT, she ordered. Her eyes filled with tears. KNOCK IT OFF. Maddie wiped her nose across her coat, and walked toward the school steps.

Chapter Sixteen

Teacher's pet
Teacher's pet
Meow meow meow
Charlie's as smart
As a big dumb cow.

Charlie leaned against his locker still wearing his drippy boots. There hadn't been any notes for two days. Maybe, he had dared to hope, they'd finally stopped. Maybe it was somebody else's turn now. But then there was this one, big as a billboard, hanging where everybody, including Mrs. Lewis, the crossing guard, could see. Luckily it was such a cold day that there weren't too many walkers, and the ones he saw buried their faces in their scarves. Still, you never knew.

Charlie bit the spot inside his cheek that was

now raw and puckered. It was a secret spot, and even though it stung when his teeth tugged it, it was comforting and familiar, the way the Goodies were when he arranged them on the windowsill at night. Still, this note. The worst one of all. For anyone to read. It was much worse than getting your name on the blackboard—not that Charlie had firsthand experience.

Kids rushed past him like nothing was different, and Charlie turned his head left and then right, like he was watching a tennis match.

"Charlie!" a voice called. Charlie turned around. It was Thomas, gesturing for him. "Come on," he called, his red hair vivid under the fluorescent light. Charlie opened his mouth to answer, but nothing came out. Not a word. Not a syllable. Thomas looked at him as if he didn't understand, then disappeared inside the classroom.

But suddenly Charlie's heart stopped pounding. He knew what to do. NEW RULE, Charlie decided. NO MORE TALKING. If he didn't talk, then nobody would ever have a reason to pick on him. No more raising his hand in class, not even if nobody else could name all seven continents or tell the difference between stalactites and stalagmites. No volunteering to clap the erasers at the end of the day or take messages to the principal's office.

Charlie smiled as he slipped into his seat and listened to the morning announcements. Lunch:

chili con carne. Open house Thursday at seven P.M. Permission slips for the field trip to the Science Museum due tomorrow. He didn't move until Mrs. Anderson asked everybody to get their reading folders from their cubbies.

"Hi, Charlie." Jessica smiled as she passed. "I like your terrarium." She pointed at the glass container Charlie had brought in the other day, complete with moss and mushrooms he had purchased with his allowance at the greenhouse. Already fat dots of condensation were forming, and a new mushroom had sprouted. Charlie looked at her and didn't say a word.

"Well, you're rude," she said. "Mrs. Anderson says we're supposed to be a kind community. You're not doing like she asked. I'm telling Mrs. Anderson—"

"Shut up, Jessica," he hissed. He tried to walk past her, but she followed close behind.

"You're not allowed to say that in school. I could tell on you."

"Jessica," he warned her, without turning around, "if you don't get out of my way, you're going to be sorry."

"Something physical?" she said. "We're not allowed to be physical in school, Charlie."

"Don't tempt me," he said, and he sat down.

PROTAGONIST, Mrs. Anderson wrote on the blackboard. "Who can tell me what a protagonist is?"

Not one hand went up.

"Charlie?" Mrs. Anderson asked hopefully. "Can you help us out?"

Charlie shook his head.

"Do you feel all right, Charlie?" she asked.

Charlie shrugged his shoulders and pretended to be taking notes, even though what he was really writing was SHUT UP SHUT UP SHUT UP over and over again in one skinny line down the page.

Chapter Seventeen

Jessica leaned across her pink-and-white-striped pillow and faced Karen. She held out the note.

Watch your step
You better run
We're not even
Nearly done.

"What do you think?" she asked.

"Watch your step? That's pathetic," Karen said. "Isn't that what it says before you get on an escalator?"

"I thought it sounded mysterious." Maddie's voice was muffled. Jessica was letting her try on her clothes, and Maddie was pulling a turtleneck with black sparkly zigzags over her head.

"Well, it doesn't," Karen said as she looked at Jessica. "Personally," Karen continued, "I think notes are boring. Don't you?"

"I don't know." Jessica sat up cross-legged and put a magazine on her lap. "What do you think, Maddie?"

Maddie was struggling to button Jessica's black jumper. She stopped and looked at them.

So this was how it would end. Even though she'd worked hard on some of those notes—harder even than on her homework—she didn't mind admitting they were boring if it meant she wouldn't have to write them anymore. And it was true: Charlie didn't seem bothered by them any longer. She'd watched his face after he got her last masterpiece, the one that read

Knock knock.
Who's there?
Lou.
Lou who?
Loser.

All he'd done was stuff it into his pocket and go back to his history reading with that little smile he always had on his face these days.

"I agree," Maddie said. "I think we should stop."

"I didn't say we should stop," Karen said. "That's not at all what I said. I like torturing Charlie." For the first time, she turned directly to Maddie. "Don't you?"

"I guess," Maddie said slowly, staring at her nails.

"Maybe," said Jessica, suddenly sitting up straight,

"we could make him do things. Dangerous things. Things that would really get him in trouble. Like stealing Mrs. Anderson's purse from her desk."

"That's what I was thinking," said Karen.

Maddie looked at them. "Charlie would never steal."

"She still likes him," said Karen. "See what I mean?" And her little eyes got even littler, until all that was left were two black dots, small as raisins.

"No."

"You want to marry him," Karen said, and she tilted her head upward so that Maddie could see deep inside her wide nostrils.

"I do not."

"Charlie and Maddie sitting in a tree, K-I-S-S-I-N-G—"

"Karen—" Jessica started to say.

"She doesn't have to do anything," Karen went on, as if Maddie wasn't even in the room. "It's not like we're making her."

Jessica looked at Maddie and waited.

I could pretend I'm sick to my stomach, Maddie thought. Or I could faint. She'd heard about people who could do that—hold their breath until there was no more oxygen in their brains and then pass out.

"It's got to be something he hates," she heard herself say. "Something scary."

"Like what, Maddie? You tell us," Jessica urged

in that voice soft as music that Maddie could never refuse. "Maddie?"

"Heights." Maddie said at last. "Charlie's scared of heights." She could hardly breathe, but the words tumbled out before she could stop them.

"Heights," repeated Jessica with a sweet smile. She clucked her tongue and shook her head. And then she walked over to her desk and pulled out a metal tin decorated with a wreath of teddy bears and hearts. "Gummi Bear?" she asked.

Chapter Eighteen

Charlie's room was nearly dark. Only the big flashlight—the one his parents kept on hand in case there was a power failure—glowed. He had already put on his pajamas, brushed his teeth, and kissed his parents good night. He was pretty sure they were convinced he was tired and wouldn't interrupt.

He walked to the windowsill. "Today's your big day, Freckles," he said, and he gently lifted the Freckles Goodie out of its cigar-box doghouse and carried it to his desk. Egypt was this year's museum unit, and Charlie was especially interested in burial customs.

He dipped the Freckles Goodie in a plastic container of water, and then rolled it in salt. "There. Now you're preserved forever," he whispered.

As he cut the old pillowcase he'd found in the laundry room into thin strips, he thought about his parents. He knew they were worried about him. He could tell, because whenever he had to say something, even something dumb like "Pass the green beans," they stopped whatever they were doing and listened closely, as if the future of the world was at stake. His mother would open the door to his room just a crack, and even though he pretended not to see, he could feel her eyes on his back. She'd study him when he was reading or doing his homework or even watching TV.

Charlie wound the strips carefully around Freckles's legs and paws and remembered how they bugged and bugged him about having a birthday party, which he kept telling them he didn't want. What was the big deal? Sure he liked presents. A camera was what he'd hinted at for weeks, even though he knew it was pretty unlikely. He'd even take ice cream and cake, as long as the icing wasn't that sticky-sweet stuff on the supermarket cakes. But no party.

Charlie wrapped the next pile of strips around Freckles's stomach and head. "All your vital organs have been removed, Freckles, except for your heart, of course."

His parents would never understand that he wasn't able to have a party, now that his latest rule didn't allow talking. He bet that would worry them so much that they'd probably sneak around his room when he wasn't at home and find the notes. They might even call Dr. Hubert, the school psychologist, and make an appointment to figure out what his problem was.

His mother made a million suggestions: a swimming party at the Y, a bowling party, even a make-your-own-pizza party, which might have held some interest for Charlie under different circumstances.

"We'll make real dough out of yeast, and all your friends can shape their dough any way they like. And I'll have lots of toppings. Pepperoni and mushroom and different kinds of cheeses. Just like in a real restaurant. How's that sound?"

"No thank you." Charlie shook his head.

"Can your father and I at least take you out to Luigi's?" Luigi's was Charlie's favorite restaurant in the world. "The first double-digit birthday is a biggie," she added, as if he didn't know.

"I guess," he told her.

"Is there anyone special you'd like to invite?"

"No," he said, "No. No. No"—before they even had a chance to mention Maddie.

Charlie looked down at the Freckles Goodie. Not one feature—not even Freckles's pointy little ears—peeked through. He was a perfect mummy.

"And now, Freckles," Charlie declared, "you are officially ready for your royal burial."

* * *

The three of them went to Luigi's, and his father ordered an antipasto to share, and then Charlie twirled his linguini with white clam sauce around his spoon. "It's his birthday," his mother kept repeating to whoever happened to be nearest: the hostess who took them to their seats, the waiter, even the tiny old guy who filled their water glasses. Charlie ate quickly, hoping he could make the meal end sooner, but no, his father wanted another glass of wine, and his mother needed a cup of tea with lemon because she thought she was getting a cold. Finally the tiny old guy cleared the table, but much to Charlie's horror, the entire staff of waiters materialized holding a huge wedge of strawberry cheesecake with a candle stuck in the center. They sang "Happy Birthday to You," drawing out the last "You" in an elaborate harmony. He hid his face with his napkin as everybody in the restaurant applauded.

At last they were home, and Charlie could open his presents. A wallet and a pair of pajamas from his grandmother ("She means well," his mother said), a mechanical pencil from his parents, and yes, a camera. It was compact enough to fit neatly in his hand, and it had a flash and an automatic focus, just like Charlie wanted. He watched as his father showed him how to load the film.

Suddenly the doorbell rang.

"That's strange," his mother said. "A little late,

isn't it?" She walked to the door and flicked on the porch light. "Well, well, well, who have we here!" he heard her shout, and then the door opened, and there were footsteps, and then he saw Maddie, standing in his living room, with a small package wrapped in purple tissue paper.

Chapter Nineteen

"Are you going to talk?" Maddie asked, as she followed Charlie upstairs. "Because you never say anything these days."

Charlie shrugged his shoulders.

"I was going to wait until morning," Maddie continued, "but my mother said that a birthday present wasn't a birthday present if you didn't get it on your real birthday. Open it."

"Later," Charlie said. "Besides, I can kind of guess what it is." Maddie followed his eyes as he looked at the Goodies lined up neatly on his windowsill.

"What happened to them?" she asked.

"They're mummies," he replied.

"But you can't tell what they look like." She lifted Freckles and picked at the corner of fabric. She found the end and began to unravel it.

"Leave it alone," Charlie said, so she set it back down.

Maddie looked around. Nothing had changed. Not the red ginger-jar lamp or the microscope and science experiments on top of the bookshelf or the board games stacked neatly on their shelf. The long view across the lawn from his window, the nubby feel of the beige-and-green-plaid bedspread, even the smell—a mixture of clean clothes and furniture polish—was as familiar to Maddie as her own room. Only Charlie, who sat silently, watching her, was different.

"What's that?" she asked, as he sat on the floor and pulled a folder out from under his bed.

"I want to show you something."

He opened the folder and laid out the notes, which were written on all different sizes of paper, from big sheets of construction paper to ragged scraps. He pieced them together neatly into a huge kind of crazy quilt.

Maddie stood absolutely still and watched. I'm a girl in a movie, she told herself. *Quiet on the set,* the director shouted. *Lights, camera, action!*

"Did you ever see so many stupid notes?" Charlie asked.

Look down, the director told her. *Look at all those notes!*

Charlie has bad breath.

Charlie has cooties.

Charlie is a chicken.

She'd tried to disguise her handwriting.

"I know who they're from," Charlie said. "I could tell right away—"

Maddie swept her hands across the pages and gathered them into a big pile.

"Hey," Charlie said. "I'm not done."

She stood and pulled up her knee socks. "Just forget about them, Charlie," she said.

"Forget about them?" He looked at her like she was speaking a foreign language. "Forget about them?" he repeated.

"They're not true," she said. "They're just made up." She didn't look at him. She reached for a ball-point pen from his desk and drew thick stripes that she knew she'd never be able to wash off around the rubber rims of her new sneakers.

"I know that, Maddie," Charlie told her, in a flat voice that she didn't recognize. "But what I don't know is why you're friends with them. That's what I don't understand. I thought you were different." He stood over her with his hands folded across his chest like a giant in his kingdom and kicked the pile of notes so they lifted in the air and then gently settled on the floor.

"I think I'm late," Maddie said.

"Don't forget your coat," Charlie said, and threw it so hard that the metal buckle flicked hard across Maddie's mouth.

"That hurt," she said.

"Sorry," he replied, but she could tell he didn't mean it.

"Happy birthday," Maddie said, and she didn't even bother to put on her coat as she ran out the attic door and down the stairs.

Chapter Twenty

Charlie closed the door to his bedroom. He could hear Maddie two floors below, talking to his parents.

The box Maddie had been carrying was lying on the floor, half hidden by his bedspread. Charlie picked it up and tugged its blue ribbon. It unfurled and then bounced back when he let go.

The box was light and rectangular. Maybe it was a Goodie goose, or a tree. He remembered late fall, the very last time Maddie had come over. The mountains were no longer golden and red but had turned nearly all brown. Maddie had scrambled halfway up the pine tree and shouted at a flock of Canada geese that were flying overhead in a perfect V formation: "Have a nice vacation! Don't forget your sunblock!"

That afternoon seemed like a billion centuries ago.

Charlie tore one small corner of the tissue paper

and then another, at the opposite corner. Then he ripped open the rest of the paper and opened the lid of the box, and the present dropped into his lap.

A foxtail. A ball with a long silk tail that fluttered like a comet when you threw it. It was the kind of gift mothers picked out when they went to the toy store without you, or a grab-bag gift for a kid you didn't even know that well.

Maddie, who always gave Charlie a Goodie, and who made other people masks, finger puppets, clay beads—all kinds of things because she said she didn't believe in store-bought presents—had given Charlie a foxtail.

Charlie put on his shoes, tucked the foxtail into his pants pocket, and walked downstairs.

"Charlie! Join the party!" his father said as he stirred a pot of cocoa on the stove. Maddie sat on a stool next to him. Charlie walked past her.

"And where do you think you're going at this time of night?" his mother said.

"To look at the moon." He wrapped his long striped scarf around his neck over and over again, until all that was left were two fringed ends that stuck straight out.

"Now?" his mother asked.

"We're supposed to. We're studying the solar system. Remember?"

"Come back soon," his father said, and then added, "Aren't you going to wait for Maddie?"

Charlie shrugged his shoulders and walked ahead, but he could hear Maddie's footsteps behind him.

He walked across the lawn. The grass, crusty with frost, crunched under his feet.

"Where are you going, Charlie?" He could hear Maddie breathing hard. For once she had to try to keep up with him.

Charlie reached the pine tree, pulled the foxtail out of his pocket, and juggled it between his two palms for a minute.

"We can't play catch," Maddie said. "The moon's not that bright."

With a snap of his elbow, Charlie hurled the foxtail overhead into the tree, but it came down again and grazed his head.

"What are you doing, Charlie?" Maddie asked. Charlie turned and was about to tell her to back off, but she was already motionless, still as the silhouette of a tree.

Charlie tried again, and this time he threw so hard that his elbow ached. And the foxtail stayed.

"Why did you do that?" Maddie cried. She walked to the base of the tree and looked up into the blackness. "Go get it!"

Charlie faced her. "I'll never get it," he said in a measured, soft voice, "because I don't like to climb. You know that, Maddie."

"Then I'll get it," she said. "Tomorrow morning

before school. It's mine. I had to spend half my allowance on it."

"Private property," Charlie told her. "No trespassing." He walked swiftly toward the house.

"You're not being nice, Charlie!" Maddie screamed after him. "That was a birthday present."

Charlie stepped into the bright kitchen and took off his coat and scarf.

That's that, he thought. The foxtail can stay there forever. He took a few sips of hot chocolate, kissed his parents good night, and walked upstairs. There he swept the Goodies off his windowsill into a plastic bag and kicked the bag far under his bed. Good, he told himself. Goody. They're stupid and babyish and do nothing but take up important space.

Chapter Twenty-one

Charlie felt like a medieval guy with the plague. All around him kids were laughing and whispering or looking at each other's projects, but nobody came near him.

His eyes followed Maddie as she removed a black-velvet headband with gold stars from her hair and put it back in place. She was standing next to the terrarium projects. In fact, she was peering inside Charlie's. He knew she wanted to open it. Sure enough, she put her hand over the lid. Don't you dare, he thought, and as if she could read his mind, she took her hand from the lid and walked away.

Mrs. Anderson stood in front of the room and clapped her hands. "Slow down," she said to some boys who were already racing to get to the front of the line for art class. "First, you need to go to your lockers and get your smocks."

Charlie waited until everyone left before he stood up.

"Everything okay?" Mrs. Anderson asked him, in the chirpy voice grown-ups used when they were trying to hide the fact that they were worried.

"Sure," Charlie said, and he scooted ahead of her.

Charlie opened his locker and reached for his smock, neatly folded on the top shelf where wet paint or clay residue wouldn't get on his schoolwork. He was just about to slam the locker shut when he saw it, rolled up and tied to the hook with a red ribbon. He'd been sure the notes were over—the last one was over a week ago, thumbtacked to a telephone pole.

Charlie unraveled it. It looked like a pirate's treasure map, with singed edges and skulls and crossbones in all four corners. But the halls had cleared out, and he was already late for art, so he rolled it up and waited until he got home.

A treasure hunt is lots of fun.
Just follow the clues
and then we're all done.
We bet you can't do it,
but if you do,
we'll stop writing notes
and you'll find a prize, too.

Charlie was tempted to toss the map into his garbage pail. It looked like a baby board game, with its twists and turns. Like Candy Land, maybe, or Chutes and Ladders. But then he studied it. Some buildings were labeled, like the school and the library, but there was also a code in the corner. A triangle meant a tree. Dotted lines equaled paved road. A black circle meant Dead End.

"What's that?" Charlie's mother asked. She stood behind him with her hands on his shoulders.

"A treasure map."

"Did you make it?" she asked.

"Nope."

"Then who did?"

"Jessica McGuire."

"And why did Jessica McGuire give you a treasure map?" She waited a couple of seconds and then snapped her fingers in front of his face. "Charlie!"

"What?" He looked up.

"You're on another planet these days. Why did Jessica McGuire give you a treasure map?"

To make me crazy, he could've said. Instead, he lied: "It's homework. Map reading. We all have to make treasure maps for each other."

"And who did you choose?"

"Thomas."

Charlie put on his helmet and rode to the end of the block. The first clue was a blue circle with the word *Lagoon* printed underneath.

It's a pipe for the sewer.
Yuck. Yuck. Yuck. Yuck.
You better wear boots—
Unless you're a duck.

"Piece of cake," Charlie said out loud. He walked across the street to the new house that was under construction. The water that filled the foundation had frozen over, and the other day when Charlie had walked past, some junior high kids were playing ice hockey.

Charlie studied the map again, following the arrow to a hot-dog shape. He looked down at the piles of warped plywood and dented soda cans wedged in the frozen mud. And then he saw it: a long, rust-colored sewer pipe that ran the full length of the foundation.

He knelt down and peered through the opening. Far away at the other end he could see a tiny circle of light. He put on his mittens and crawled into the pipe. With every inch forward the cold, hard cement pounded against his hands and knees. He thought about standing upright and wobbling like a penguin but realized that, even bent down low, he wouldn't fit. Slowly he made his way forward, stopping every few inches to catch his breath. Finally, he reached the end and tumbled out onto the gravel. And there, waving like a flag on a stick right in front of him, was the next clue:

Ride to the fountain that
bubbles in spring.
Look for the next clue
near the cement thing.

Another lousy rhyme, Charlie thought. Not to mention a lousy clue. He knew exactly where he was supposed to go and looked at his watch. "Ten minutes. Fifteen at the most," he calculated, "and I'll be done."

The only fountain was the one in front of the library. And the cement thing was this circle on the ground that he used to think was a pet's grave, until the librarian told him it was a planter some rich guy donated years ago.

He leaned forward and pushed against the handlebars, as if that would make his three-speed go faster, but the tires spun on the ice and he had to walk the bike over to where the road had been sanded and he could gain traction.

For a second Charlie thought it was just a plastic bag that had blown into the center of the circle, but when he opened it up, he saw the clue, cut into pieces. Charlie spread them on top of the bag and fit them together.

It's orange and twisty,
And the clue's at the top.
But first close your eyes
And hop hop hop hop.

Forget it, Charlie told himself. Try and make me. The sun had just fallen behind the mountains, and instantly it was colder. Charlie put his hands under his armpits and looked about. Nobody was in sight, unless you counted the lady coming down the library steps holding a canvas bag.

Charlie got back on his bike and rode to the swirly slide at the far corner of the school playground. He carefully made his way up the four metal bars that served as a ladder, and there it was, sticking out of a crack in the wooden platform:

Open the door
That leads to the gym.
You'll find your clue under
The basketball rim.

Charlie stuck his hand into the back pocket of his blue jeans and felt around. Then he pulled out a squished box of rainbow-colored Chiclets. He could see through the cellophane window that there were only three left, and he shook the box until they tumbled out into his hand and he popped them into his mouth.

He sucked on the Chiclets until the smooth candy coating became rough like a cat's tongue. Then he chewed hard and looked around. The dark clouds and the mountains overlapped, so it was hard to tell where one ended and the other began. The wood-burning stoves sent a bluish haze spiraling down into the valley. And he could see, far away, the smoke-stacks from the shoe factory one town over, with their rings of tiny red lights all around the tops to warn small planes that flew into the local airport.

There were still a few cars in the parking lot. Probably Mrs. Anderson was there, in her classroom, writing the next day's lessons on the blackboard.

Charlie opened the heavy double doors to the gym and stepped inside. The light that filtered through the high windows over the bleachers was dim, and the four basketball nets at each end hung like tired ghosts. Charlie stepped on the black outline and followed it under the first two basketball hoops until he reached the third, and saw the note, written on a piece of yellow construction paper, taped to the floor. He picked it up and coughed, and the sound reverberated against the cement block walls.

The last clue is the best of all.
First you have to walk down the hall.
Go to the multipurpose room and
climb the stairs to the roof.
Now stand in the middle.
Your prize will be waiting
because you solved the riddle.
The notes will end and that is true.
This is the last time we bug you!

Charlie opened the door to the gym that led into the front hallway. It looked like a tunnel, and he walked on his tiptoes as he passed the map outside the gym with its black magic marker line that inched across the United States, documenting all the miles each class ran during phys. ed. There was the dinosaur mural and the quilt for the PTO raffle, the recycling containers, and the lost-and-found bin, filled with coats and gloves and lunch boxes.

Something hard gave a shudder and Charlie jumped. Then it happened again. Charlie stood still and looked around. It was just the pipes overhead. They probably clanged all day, but you couldn't hear them over all the noise. For one second Charlie heard voices, like soft laughter. But then they stopped.

The sooner I do this, the sooner it'll be all over, Charlie thought, and he started to run—long, silent leaps like an antelope across the speckled linoleum floor. He ran down the ramp to the multipurpose room and through the doors, and up the wooden steps to the stage.

Charlie pulled apart the heavy velvet curtains in the middle and stepped backstage. The fluorescent lights in the auditorium didn't reach back here; the only light was a dim red bulb that was high above, near the catwalk where Mr. Kittler climbed when he was adjusting the lights for a talent show or a concert. Charlie saw the stairs in the far corner of the stage.

They weren't much higher than the stairs to his attic room.

He walked over and ran his hands along the smooth, cold metal, and went up the first step, and then the next. His body felt strong as a mountain climber's as he climbed higher and higher.

And then he was there, at the very top. He unhooked the latch and pushed gently on the trapdoor, but it didn't budge. He tried again, harder this time. Finally, he could feel the door open, but then it slammed shut. He tried again, but this time he used his head as well as his hand to pry it open. Suddenly there was a rush of cold night air, and he could hear the hatch as its hinge swung over and it smacked against the blacktop roof.

Charlie climbed out and walked carefully to the middle. He could see the spiral slide from here, but it looked small and far away. He felt light as a snowflake: If he spread his arms, he might be lifted gently above the roof by an air current and deposited on his own doorstep.

Okay, where's the stupid prize? Charlie asked himself. He wanted to get this over with, to go home and eat the macaroni and cheese his mother was probably taking out of the oven right that second.

He heard voices again—the same ones he'd heard a few minutes before—only this time he knew they were real.

"I know you're here, Jessica," he said, "so you might as well come out."

Suddenly there was a loud sound, more like a thud than a bang, and then laughter. When Charlie turned, he saw that the hatch door was closed. He bent down and tried to lift it.

It was locked.

Charlie stood and walked to the middle, away from the dark edges of the roof. A large poster board leaned against the air duct, held in place by a rock. He walked over to the sign.

DEAR CHARLIE,

GETTING UP WAS THE EASY PART. HOW ARE YOU GOING TO GET DOWN?

Chapter Twenty-two

Maddie was getting organized. She opened her top desk drawer and cleaned out old scraps of paper and crayons and pencils too stubby to use. She tested her Magic Markers and threw away the ones that had dried out. She wiped the top of her desk with a damp washcloth until it shone.

Next, Maddie lay on her stomach and looked under her bed. She pulled out all the dusty socks and board games and stuffed animals that had accumulated. If the rest of the house was a mess, at least her room would be in order. She vowed to save her allowance and buy a padlock so nobody could come in unless they were invited.

"Maddie, come out from under there, please."

Maddie slid from under the bed and sat up.

"Charlie's mom just called," Josie said. The little worry lines in between Josie's eyes were even deeper than usual. "She said Charlie went out before dinner and he's not back yet. She's worried to death."

Maddie thought of Charlie following the clues and a cold feeling settled in her chest, like when you swallow ice cream and it goes down the wrong way.

"He's not here, is he? Hiding in your closet?"

"Of course not."

"Then why are you smiling?"

"I can't help it. I'm worried."

"You're worried, so you smile. It's a horrible habit."

"Sorry."

Josie's voice softened. "She wondered if you knew anything about Charlie."

"No!" Maddie said. She looked at the alarm clock on her night table. It was after seven. It never should have taken him this long, she thought. Stupid Charlie. You were supposed to be such a good map reader. What'd you do? Chicken out? She could picture him hiding in the supply closet, next to the stacks of lined paper. He probably took along a book and a flashlight and was eating a stash of candy bars and laughing at them.

But then another picture took shape. It covered the old picture like a collage until all that was left was Charlie crouching, but this time he was on a ladder and he was slipping and his arms were flailing like a windmill and then he hit the black macadam down below.

Maddie looked at Josie. Go away, she pleaded

silently. Go, so I can go and bring Charlie home.

"Janet said something about a treasure map. Some school project." Josie opened Maddie's jewelry box and juggled a beaded necklace between her hands.

DEMERITS FOR TALKING IN CLASS. BUTTON YOUR LIPS. IS WHAT YOU HAVE TO SAY SO IMPORTANT IT CAN'T WAIT UNTIL RECESS? RESPECT OTHER PEOPLE'S PERSONAL PROPERTY, Maddie wanted to scream, but instead she said, "Don't touch. You're always touching my things."

Josie put the necklace back in its box and rested her palm on her cheek as if she'd been slapped. "I'm going," she stated in that flat, quiet voice she used when she was truly angry. "And please try to think of where Charlie is." She paused, and for a second Maddie thought she was going to come over and put her arms around her. But she shook her head, turned, and closed the door behind her.

Chapter Twenty-three

Charlie breathed in too deeply and started coughing. He wondered if anybody had ever choked on air. He jiggled the metal handle again, but it was no use. The door was locked, and the flag on the roof snapped like a cap gun.

He crawled on his knees, closer and closer to the edge of the roof. The ladder was clamped to the brick wall. He lay on his stomach with his face pressed against the smooth surface, remembering last summer, when the roof was being redone and the acrid smell of thick, sticky tar hung in the air around the playground.

The railing curved on either side like a waterfall. It seemed like if you entered the black space between the rails, you'd be doomed and cascade down, like a guy in a barrel going over Niagara Falls. Charlie closed his eyes tightly and opened them again and reached. His fingertips could go through the railing and just touch the top metal rung.

Something cracked. Charlie waited, and then the crackling sound started again. He sat up and looked around and then realized the source: Icicles were dropping to the ground, as though they were being plucked by an invisible hand. He crawled backward toward the middle of the roof and lay on his back, shivering. High above, the sky was filled with stars.

Compared to the entire universe, he thought, I should be able to climb down one stupid ladder. I hope you're watching.

There were voices and laughter down below, in the parking lot. Footsteps. Car doors slamming shut, and engines starting. Four headlights far below, and then a serpentine of light, sharp and clear at first, as the cars went into reverse and then forward.

Find me! Charlie pleaded silently. I don't care if I get detention. Find me! He could hear a muffled bass from one of the cars' radios, and then silence and dark, like a blanket pulled over his face, as the cars turned onto School Street and were gone.

Again, he crawled over to the ladder, and when he was close enough to touch it, he turned around. Looking over his shoulder, he backed up slowly, until he could grip the railing, first with one hand, and then with the other. The railing was cold, and Charlie wished he had put his mittens on first, but it was too late. He couldn't let go.

Only two feet of empty air, he calculated, stood between him and the ladder. Two feet. He swung one leg and then the other through the empty space, and could feel the edge of the rung with his toes, but then he slipped and dangled for a second in the empty air until his feet found the thin metal rung again. He held tight as if a tornado could come along and rip him away. Then he looked down. The yellow light over the door down below shone on the ladder, and he could see that it was covered with a slick coating of ice.

He hummed. "Go Tell Aunt Rhody" was the first thing that came to mind, maybe because they had practiced it in band class on their recorders the other day. And then he lowered himself to the next rung, and the one after that. The roof was in front of him now.

His fingers were numb with cold. "That's enough," he said aloud. "It's time to go home. One foot in front of the other. They're steep stairs. Take your time, Charlie. You've got all the time in the world."

He needed a rule. Something to make him look straight ahead at the brick wall instead of down, into that cavern of air. Three short inhales, one long exhale, every time he stepped down. Inhale, inhale, inhale, long exhale.

His foot touched something hard and gravelly. Charlie lowered his other foot but still held on tight. He turned his head. The door to the gym, the monkey bars, the swings—they were all at eye level now.

Charlie looked up. The ladder reached into the sky, overlapping with the stars.

He was down.

When Charlie finally walked through the door, his mother kissed him so many times he lost count and his father hugged him so hard it hurt.

Later that night, after Charlie ate two bowls of minestrone soup and soaked in a very hot tub, he lay in bed. His body was tired, but he couldn't stop his brain from retracing the treasure hunt's route. He rubbed his cheek across the flannel pillowcase and could feel himself falling—not the fall he had imagined a few hours ago, his body piercing through space—but another fall, more of a tumble, into something thick and soft, like pom-pom balls. He hovered on the edge, just ready to dive in, when his body shuddered and he opened his eyes.

Charlie had climbed down a ladder as high as any tree. He had done this all by himself, and the only person in the world who knew what that meant had given him a foxtail for his birthday and couldn't care less.

Chapter Twenty-four

Maddie picked up the shoe box, set it gently in the bottom of her backpack, and finished getting dressed for school.

She was holding the box in her hands by the time Mrs. Anderson gave the signal to line up. She pretended she didn't see Jessica waving to catch her attention and stayed behind, waiting for Charlie, who was leaning over, looking inside his terrarium.

"There's new moss," Maddie said, and Charlie looked up, surprised. "Sorry. I didn't mean to scare you," she said.

"You didn't." Charlie opened the lid of his desk and pulled out his lunch bag. He walked toward the door.

"Charlie," Maddie said, "I have something for you."

Charlie stopped but didn't turn around.

"Here," she said. "I got up early to make it. It's not much, but it's your REAL birthday present." She handed him the shoe box and waited.

"You already gave me a foxtail." Why was she giving this to him?

"That didn't count. Aren't you going to open it?"

"Maybe later." He shook the box and heard something bump against the cardboard sides.

"Let me know how you like it," Maddie said.

Charlie nodded once.

"What is it?" Thomas asked.

"A bologna sandwich." Charlie slid his sandwich out of the plastic bag and held it up.

"Not that," said Thomas. "That." And he pointed to the shoe box on the table.

"It's nothing," Charlie answered.

"Can I have the box?" Thomas reached in front of him and grabbed it before Charlie could protest. "It's a good size."

"No," said Charlie. He took one bite of his sandwich and set it down. The bologna stood out, pink and rubbery, against the white bread. Charlie's stomach churned.

"Hey, there's something inside." Thomas opened the lid before Charlie could say anything and pulled out a little round shape with two wings tilted upward and a tiny beak. It was hard on the outside, but when Charlie squeezed it a little, he could tell that it hadn't dried completely. It was a bird—a Goodie bird.

Charlie handed the box to Thomas and held the Goodie in the palm of his closed hand. It already felt like an old friend.

Chapter Twenty-five

"Hey, Charlie! CHARLIE!" Jessica McGuire caught up with Charlie at the end of the day, just before she had to run to get her bus. She cupped her hand around Charlie's ear and whispered: "I have a secret."

"I have to go, Jessica." Charlie started to pull away, but she grabbed the sleeve of his coat.

"It's a good secret. It's about those notes."

"Go away, Jessica. I'm busy." Charlie waved his hand and wished it was a flyswatter that could shoo her away.

"I know who wrote them."

She wasn't going to let him leave. He could see that. He tapped his foot impatiently. "Who, Jessica?"

"Maddie."

"Sure, Jessica. Right." Charlie studied Jessica's nose, which tilted upward. He imagined flicking its tip with his finger.

Jessica sounded apologetic. "I told her not to, but she did anyway."

"She did not."

"She did too. You can ask her yourself if you don't believe me." She grabbed his arm, and Charlie pulled away.

"Leave me alone, Jessica."

"I'm just trying to be nice." Her eyes darted around, as if she was searching for Karen.

"Yeah. Right."

"I am."

He almost felt sorry for her; he could almost believe her. But then she continued: "No wonder nobody likes you."

"Leave me alone, Jessica." ABRACADABRA! GONE!

"You're always mean to me," she said.

"Takes one to know one."

"Two years ago I invited you to my birthday party, and you didn't even come."

"You did not."

"I did too. And you never want to be in my reading circle, even though we're always on the same level."

Jessica kept speaking, but the words didn't make sense. They ricocheted like pinballs inside his head.

Maddie?

"That's the problem with you, Charlie Siegel," Jessica said. "You think you know everything."

Charlie is a chicken.

"What are you talking about?"

"You should be mad at Maddie. Not me. Who cares about you, anyway?"

Maddie wrote the notes.

"Besides, did I tell you my father's taking me to Disney World for spring vacation? So there." She jabbed her forefinger into his chest as she spoke the final two words, and then she walked away.

Chapter Twenty-six

"Charlie!" his mother called, but Charlie didn't bother to answer. He had something important to do and didn't have time for distractions.

"Charlie!" she called again, but he ignored her. "Charlie! Why didn't you answer me? That's not like you." She stood in the doorway to his room with a worried expression.

"Sorry," he said. "I didn't hear you."

"You didn't hear me? Maybe you need to get your ears cleaned." He looked at her and she was smiling. "How was your day?" she asked.

Charlie almost told her everything: how Maddie had lied to him about the notes, how those horrible girls had tortured him—*him,* out of all the boys in his class!—with those notes. His mother would be so nice. She'd listen and rub his back and probably tell him that all friendships have their ups and downs and that if he could ignore those girls, they'd probably get bored and leave him alone.

But he couldn't. He felt sorry for his mother, having a son like him.

The phone rang in his parents' bedroom. His mother held up her index finger. "Don't move," she said. He could hear her talking and then she came back, holding the phone.

"It's Maddie," she said. "She wants to talk to you."

Charlie shook his head.

"Honey, she's waiting."

"No," he told her. "No. No. No. Can't you see I'm busy?"

His mother turned back and spoke into the phone. Then she listened for a few seconds before saying "Okay, Maddie, I'll tell him," and hung up. "She said you should call her later. Charlie?"

"I have lots of homework."

"Can't it wait?"

"I want to do it now," he said.

His mother walked toward the door and turned around. "I'm downstairs if you need me," she said.

An alien occupied Charlie's body. He looked at himself in the mirror and was surprised to see that he looked the same. He stuck out his tongue. What was he expecting—for it to be blue with purple polka dots? He felt his forehead. Why was he so hot? He opened the windows and leaned out. Too bad Maddie wasn't walking right below, he thought. She'd make a perfect spitting target. He spit just the same, aiming for a Siamese cat he didn't recognize that was crossing the sidewalk.

I am different, he thought. I didn't even let my father spray the red ants under the porch last summer, and here I am spitting at stray cats.

Charlie sat down at his desk and took a piece of white paper from his neat stack. The old Charlie would have thought for a while, maybe done a rough draft or two, making sure his penmanship was perfect. But not the new Charlie. One clean draft was all he needed:

Dear Maddie,
All is forgiven. Meet me at the pine tree tomorrow at 10 a.m. sharp. I have a special surprise for you.
Charlie

He folded the note in half and taped it shut, then wrote MADDIE on the front.

"I'm going out," he said to his mother, who was concentrating on a crossword puzzle.

"To where?"

"Maddie's. I have to give her something."

"Good," she said. "Good boy." As if she knew. She looked at her watch. "Dinner's in an hour."

"I'll be back."

"And give Maddie my love!"

He smiled to himself and pretended he didn't hear.

Chapter Twenty-seven

"Maddie!"

Maddie was just about to walk into the mudroom and put her coat on when she heard her mother calling from way upstairs. Her mother called again, this time more loudly, so she turned around. "What?" she called.

"Come here, where I can see you, please."

Maddie walked into Gideon's room, which smelled like baby lotion and diapers. Gideon was sitting in the middle of his crib completely naked, except for an undershirt on top of his head. Maddie went over to him and blew into his belly button, which made him shriek with delight.

"I need your help, sweetie," Josie said. "I have to run to the store and get more diapers."

"But Josie—" Maddie said. "Charlie's waiting for me." She looked at her watch and sure enough, it was already quarter to ten.

"I'll be right back."

"Josie—" She had to go. She had to find Charlie before it was too late. Everything was going to be all right. Maddie sank down on her knees and grabbed Josie's ankles. "Please, most beautiful, precious, beloved mother. Pretty please?" She looked up.

"My daughter the actress!" Josie bent over and kissed the top of Maddie's head.

"Josie, please, not today!" What if Charlie got tired of waiting? What if he left before everything was all better?

"Sorry, sweet thing. Now where's my purse?" Josie was always losing her purse, or her glasses, or her car keys.

"It's on the couch," Maddie said, as she pulled the stacking clown out of a wicker basket. "Hurry, please!"

By the time Maddie finally got out of the house, she was already fifteen minutes late. She hoped Charlie would wait for her. Her bike was leaning against the garage door, and she grabbed it and flew out of the driveway and down streets so familiar, she could navigate them with her eyes closed.

She didn't even bother with the kickstand; she just let her bike crash in the grass and ran to the backyard and the pine tree.

"Damn it," she said out loud, the same way Paul did when he was frustrated, saying the first word a little louder than the second. "Charlie?"

"Here I am."

She looked around, but the words sounded far away.

"I'm up here," he said, "straight above you."

She looked up and there, sure enough, was Charlie, higher even than Maddie'd ever climbed, standing on a branch of the pine tree.

"You're high!"

"No kidding."

"I got your note, so here I am!" Maddie climbed up the first few branches to join him, but Charlie called "Stop!" in a sharp voice.

"But I want to come up!" she said, and started to climb again.

"This is *my* tree. I'm the boss."

Maddie froze with one hand on a branch.

"Watch out," he called, but she didn't move. "Well, you can't say I didn't warn you. Bombs away!"

A piece of something sharp, like hail, hit her hand, and she climbed down to look more closely. "It's the Goodie Gideon! You're breaking it!" The Goodie beach ball came next. It rolled against her sneaker.

"Charlie!" She wanted to climb up the tree and make him stop, but she couldn't. All she could do was stand without moving and watch. "I didn't know you could be so mean," she called, and she put her hand in front of her face.

"Takes one to know one!" he said, as the Goodie cat fell.

One by one the Goodies plunged to the ground—the grandparents, the fireman, the cowboy, the clown. The Charlie Goodie, who snapped at the waist. The Maddie Goodie. Her head rolled next to a pinecone.

Maddie jumped back and watched. He must have unwrapped them, she thought numbly. They were mummies before.

The last thing he hurled wasn't a Goodie. It was the foxtail; its blue and red tail spun in the air like a barbershop pole. And then he stopped.

Maddie waited a few seconds, just to be sure. Then she ran around the base of the tree and gathered the broken pieces and put them in the front of her sweatshirt.

"Now I know!" he shouted.

"Know what?" Maddie called up.

"Now I know everything."

Maddie looked up. She didn't understand. It was like a riddle or a fraction problem that she knew she'd never be able to figure out.

"YOU did it." Charlie held on to the limb overhead and bounced.

"Did what, Charlie?" she asked, but suddenly she knew the answer. Her head suddenly burned, and she thought she might have a fever.

"You wrote the notes. All of them."

"What are you talking about?" She rolled her eyes the way Jessica would have, but she knew it was too late. "What notes?" She turned her back and started to walk away as if she couldn't care less.

"Stop!" Charlie shouted.

Maddie stopped.

"You know!" Charlie's voice boomed. "You knew all along! The mean notes. The ones I showed you!"

"Charlie—" She almost made something up, to pretend she didn't know what he was talking about, like the time she ate the frosting roses off Gideon's birthday cake and blamed it on the cat. "He licked it!" she'd lied to Josie. She'd even managed to make herself cry. "I tried to fix it"—she'd pointed to the places where she'd smoothed the icing over with a bread knife—"but it was hard." Her mother believed her, too—even ended up comforting her, telling her it wasn't such a big deal. Maybe Charlie would believe her. She looked at him, but his face was pinched and white with anger.

"I thought they were from Jessica, but they were really from you," Charlie yelled.

Maddie looked at Charlie. He looked older, with his legs crossed and leaning against the trunk of the tree.

"I should have guessed," he continued. "I should have recognized your crummy handwriting. And that lame treasure map—"

"Who told you?" Maddie asked. "Who?" She put her pinky in her mouth and bit the nail.

"Who do you think?"

"Charlie—"

"Catch!" he said, and he threw the new Goodie bird at her, but she missed. She looked up one more time, and then she started running.

"Pull up your knee socks," Charlie shouted after her. "You look like a baby."

Chapter Twenty-eight

When she first walked in the door, sucking on her pinky because a piece of the Goodie grandfather had cut her, Maddie thought she could escape without being detected.

But Josie was right there in the kitchen, pureeing carrots for Gideon through a little white contraption.

"Hello," Josie said. "Did you have fun?"

Maddie shrugged her shoulders.

"Could you answer me, please, when I'm talking to you?" Josie turned around, but as soon as she saw Maddie, she rushed over and put her hands on Maddie's face. "You're quiet as a mouse these days," she said. She looked closely at her face like she was reading the fine print in a book.

Maddie didn't answer. She liked the way her mother was looking at her, the way it felt to have a mystery inside that nobody could solve. Ask me, she pleaded. Go on. Ask me.

For a second Josie looked distracted; she took out a pad of paper and started making a list. Then she turned to Maddie and said, in that tone of voice Maddie loved—the one that made her feel like she was being hypnotized—"Did anyone ever tell you you have soulful eyes, Miss Maddie Muffin Martin?"

And with that she knew she was going to cry. She hardly ever cried, but whenever Josie got all soft and motherly, she couldn't help herself. And she did cry. At first, she'd have to admit, the tears were a little fake. It felt good to be sitting in Josie's lap, with Josie murmuring, "Shhh, shhh," just like she was Gideon waking from a nightmare. But then there were pictures: Jessica and that horrible follower, Karen, sitting in Jessica's room and making her write those notes; and Charlie standing like a giant in the tree. He was mean, too. Just as mean as the rest of them.

And then she cried and cried and cried until she couldn't catch her breath and she thought that she might have to throw up. Even Gideon, who was sitting on the floor sucking on a bagel, looked up at her and his face got red, like he might cry, too.

When the tears finally stopped, Josie stood and got a tissue and held it to Maddie's nose. "Blow," she said, and Maddie blew. "Now," she instructed, "here's what I want you to do. Wash your face, put on your coat, and take a nice, brisk walk around the block to clear your head." She picked up Gideon and kissed his mouth and went back to turning her carrots.

Maddie did as she was told. At first she was amazed that the planet Earth still spun in its orbit: A dog sniffed something in a bush, the mailman waved from his little white truck. A girl pedaled down the street on a pink Big Wheel.

I'm okay, I'm okay, she told herself, and she was almost convinced. It was only later, as she walked up the front steps to her house, that it occurred to her that her mother had never even asked her what it was that she was crying about. If she'd asked, Maddie would've told her that Charlie was gone forever. And it was all her fault.

Chapter Twenty-nine

Charlie lay on his back and counted the glow stars overhead. He got as high as twenty-three. Then he lost count and started all over again. He closed his eyes and pretended he was lying on the ground looking up at the sky. He imagined he could smell the damp dirt just starting to warm up and see tiny green shoots of crocuses pushing up out of the ground.

Suddenly the overhead light clicked. He opened his eyes. "Come downstairs and eat something," his father said. "We miss you."

"I'll be right there." He'd say anything if it would make his father go away. Charlie looked up again, but the comets and shooting stars had vanished.

He surveyed the room: the tropical fish tank with the colored gravel like jewels; the bulletin board with the second-place red ribbon he'd won for the sixty-yard dash during field day last May; his collection of jungle animals lined up on top of his bookshelf. And next to that: Maddie's notes.

Once they'd seemed important to save, almost like he didn't have a choice. But things were different now. He took them out of their folder and put them, one on top of the other, in a pile. Then he divided the pile into fourths and tore each pile into skinny strips. He opened his hands, and the paper fell softly onto the rug. He looked down. All he saw were parts of words, letters chopped in half. *Char, lose, tea, awa—* The notes couldn't hurt him now.

He looked closely at a moon etched in Magic Marker that shone like silver tinsel. He ran his finger across it. He should have known it was Maddie. Amazing, Charlie thought. Maddie thought of that moon. She drew it with the same hand that made the Goodies. Maybe she was lying on her quilt, looking out the window. Tickling Gideon's pudgy stomach. He missed Gideon. Same paper, same hand, same room, same baby. How could everything be the same, and yet nothing be the same?

He looked down: *si, gret, tur.* Nonsense words that meant nothing. Charlie tore the last word into six segments and walked to the bathroom. Bit by bit, so the toilet wouldn't clog, he opened his hand and let go of the piles of letters. They fell like confetti and were sucked down a tornado of water, out of sight. Five flushes. That's all it took.

"Everything all right up there, pal?" his father called.

"Fine," Charlie called back. He washed his hands and headed downstairs.

Chapter Thirty

"Close your eyes," said Jessica. She stabbed her macaroni and cheese with her fork and then took a sip of milk through her straw. "Close them," she repeated.

Maddie shut her eyes and felt something tickle her throat.

"Open!"

She looked down and fingered the little heart with a zigzag through the center.

"That's a friendship heart," Jessica said. "It means our friendship can never be broken apart."

"What about me?" said Karen. "Why don't I get a heart?"

"Because Maddie earned it. Maybe next time you'll earn one, too, Karen. You're so competitive." Jessica jabbed the last little cylinder of macaroni and smiled at Maddie.

"Next time?" Maddie asked. She looked over at Charlie. She'd tried calling him the other afternoon, but when he picked up the phone and heard her voice, he hung up. She even went to his house and rode in circles until she was dizzy, but he never came out.

She wanted to leave. She pictured herself pushing her chair away, picking up her tray, and delivering it to the cafeteria window. Walking over to Charlie and eating the spare cookie his mother used to pack for her. But her feet wouldn't move.

"Next time," Jessica said, "you'll be in charge, Maddie. Who should it be?"

"Thomas Mitkowski," said Karen. "He never washes his hair."

Jessica stood up, resting one knee on the chair. She surveyed the room. "What about a sixth grader?" she suggested. "What about Eric O'Brien? Didn't he start that whole recycling campaign thing? What do you think, Maddie? You're the note queen."

Maddie shrugged her shoulders. Suddenly she was tired. She was tired of the planning, the writing, the treasure maps; she was tired of Jessica telling her what to do, and Karen, who never liked anything she did, looking at her with eyes as slivery as two paper cuts.

"I don't know," Maddie said. She looked at the cafeteria monitor. When would she finally dismiss them?

"She doesn't want to," Karen said. "She's chickening out."

"Of course she isn't," Jessica answered. "I just gave her a present."

"Why did you choose Charlie?" Maddie asked. It went through her head—BOYS ARE BAD, GIRLS ARE GOOD—but suddenly it wasn't good enough. "Why Charlie?" she asked again.

Jessica looked at her and smiled. "Because he wouldn't be my solar system partner."

Maddie wasn't sure she'd heard right. "But you asked me first," she said.

"No, Maddie. I asked Charlie first," Jessica said in that patient voice that always made Maddie feel dumb.

"You did?"

"Yes, Maddie, I did. He's the best writer in the class." Jessica paused. "It's a free country, Maddie. Anyway," she continued, "*you* were my partner. And now you're my best friend." She looked at Karen and then turned back to Maddie. "Want my chips?" she asked.

Maddie felt sick. "No thanks," she said. Jessica continued to hold the bag up. "I don't want them."

"Why not? Do you think they're contaminated?" Karen smiled at Jessica as she tore little nuggets of bread and stuffed them into her mouth.

"So when are you going to write Eric's note?" Jessica ignored Karen and looked at Maddie.

"I'm not sure I want to," Maddie told her. "Maybe we should leave everybody alone."

"She *is* a chicken," Karen said.

"It's not like you have a choice, Maddie." Jessica squished her milk carton so it was flat.

"That's right," said Karen.

Maddie took a deep breath. "Says who, Jessica?" Maddie asked.

"Did you hear what she said?" Karen looked at Jessica, who shrugged her shoulders. "You can't say that."

"Shut up, Karen," Jessica told her. "Maddie can say whatever she wants." She flashed a bright smile.

"I think Maddie should go away," Karen said.

"Who cares what you think, Karen?" Maddie said. Don't you dare cry, she told herself, and she didn't. Her voice came out stronger this time. "Are you going to write *me* a note?"

Jessica put her arms through the sleeves of her coat. "Don't be so dramatic, Maddie," she said, and she held out her hand. "My necklace, please."

Maddie felt behind her for the latch but couldn't get it to work, so she snapped it hard and the thin chain split in two.

"Hey—" Maddie heard Jessica call, but she didn't bother to turn around.

Chapter Thirty-one

Charlie watched Maddie from his attic window. Put your helmet on the right way, you idiot, he thought. Otherwise, what's the point? He wiped his breath off the glass so he could see more clearly. She was riding in big circles right in front of his driveway, with her helmet tipped to one side and her sweatpants pulled up over her knees. Once in a while she looked up, but Charlie managed to duck each time she did.

He turned away and opened the hatch door to Sylvester's cage. Sylvester was Thomas's white rat, and Charlie was baby-sitting him for the weekend. Charlie stuck three fingers into the cage, and Sylvester sniffed his hand.

"Your tail's too long, and your eyes are too pink. Sorry, pal," he said as he lowered the hatch and went back to the window.

Maddie climbed off her bike, set it on its side

against the curb, and sat. He saw her pull something out of her pocket—a candy bar, it looked like. She tore off the orange wrapper and stuck an end of it in her mouth. He wondered where she'd gotten it. Josie never had candy in the house, even though Maddie begged for it all the time.

She was sitting on the last pile of snow left. Charlie had overheard his parents say that winter was letting go. "One more whopper," his father predicted, "and then we can get the snow tires taken off." Another winter had gone by.

Last year at this time they'd had three snow days in a row, and his father had worked all day with him and Maddie making an igloo that was big enough to hold a picnic lunch. And the next morning there'd been an ice storm. He'd heard the tree branches pop like firecrackers before he was fully awake—in fact, he'd made that sound part of a dream about the Civil War—but when he'd woken up, the world down below was covered with a clear, hard shell of ice. Maddie had called while he was still in his pajamas, eating breakfast, and told him to hurry and meet her in front of her house and to bring his ice skates, because the whole neighborhood was skating from street to street. At first his mother had said no because it was too dangerous, but then his father pulled his old skates out of the basement, and his mother found hers underneath some boxes in the front hall closet, and the three of them put them on right on their front stoop and skated down the street holding hands, with Charlie in the middle.

"Charlie!" his mother called. Charlie wrote his initials on the window.

"Charlie!" she repeated. "Maddie's downstairs."

Charlie scooted over to his bed and lay facedown, so his mother wouldn't look at his eyelids and know he was faking. He heard the door open.

"Charlie," she called. "Charlie." He heard her sigh and finally turn away.

By the time he stepped out of bed and tiptoed back over to the windowsill, Maddie was already back on her bike riding down the street with no hands.

Chapter Thirty-two

They were supposed to arrive by noon, but Josie lost the car keys so they called to say they would be a little late. They were dropping Maddie and Gideon off for the day while they went to visit Paul's aunt, who was in a nursing home. By the time they got to Charlie's house, it was the middle of the afternoon.

"Good-bye, my angel. Be a help," Josie said, as she handed Gideon to Charlie's mother and kissed Maddie over and over again. Then she got in the car, and Paul waved and honked until their car disappeared.

"Well," said Charlie's mother, "that's that. What's in there?" She touched the lid of the red shoe box Maddie was holding.

"A game," Maddie said.

"That's nice."

"Where's Charlie?" Maddie looked around.

"I don't know. He disappeared about an hour ago." She shifted Gideon to her other hip. "You're turning into a big guy, aren't you?" she said. "Why don't you try the backyard?" she said to Maddie.

Maddie walked across the open field behind Charlie's house. The ground was spongy and smelled like worms. "Charlie!" she called, but he didn't answer. "Charlie!" She heard a bird squawking overhead and when she looked up, she couldn't see Charlie—just his white socks between the branches of the tree.

"Are you going to stay there all day?" she asked.

"I might."

"Can I come up?"

"No."

"Then I'll wait for you down here," she said, and she sat on a mound of pine needles beneath the tree and held the shoe box tightly in both hands. Maddie sat and sat, until her legs started to fall asleep. Finally, something snapped and she saw Charlie move among the branches, and then he jumped to the ground next to her.

"Wait for me," she called as he walked ahead. He started to run and she did too, holding the box tightly. When she reached him, she grabbed his arm.

"Leave me alone," he said, and shook himself loose. "Go home. Who invited you, anyway?"

"I can't go home," Maddie said. "Josie and Paul just left. I have to stay here."

"Then don't talk to me."

"I won't." Maddie followed Charlie into the house. They walked through the kitchen, where his father was wearing an apron and kneading a loaf of bread.

"Hi, kids," he called. "You two look awfully conspiratorial."

Maddie smiled. Charlie didn't. She tried to keep up with him as he bolted ahead of her to the attic.

Maddie didn't move. She sat in a chair and held on to her shoe box. Charlie took out his coin collection and spread it on the floor. He made a different pile for each country—England, Scotland, Japan, Spain, Mexico. Pile after pile, like little towers. Still Maddie didn't move. Charlie didn't remember ever seeing her sit still for so long. She raised her hand.

"What?"

"Can I go to the bathroom?"

"Who do you think I am? Mrs. Anderson?"

She stood up and on the way out knocked over the Japanese coins. He put them back in a pile.

"Here," she said when she returned. She handed him the shoe box.

"What is it?" he asked.

"Open it."

He pulled off the lid.

"Go on," she said. Charlie gently lifted the white tissue paper.

And there, lying side by side in a bed of newspaper, were the Goodies.

True, almost all of them had cracks from their long fall to the ground. The dog was missing his tail, and the grandmother no longer had an arm. Charlie was missing his nose, and Maddie's forehead was chipped, but still, there they were, glued together.

"I fixed them," Maddie said. "I made Josie buy superglue, even though it never comes off your fingers."

Charlie didn't speak. He laid them back inside the box.

"You can throw them out if you want. I won't be mad," she told him.

Charlie stood up and walked over to the window.

"Where are you going?"

"Mind your own business."

Maddie picked up the shoe box and looked at the trash can under Charlie's desk. "If you don't want them, then I'm going to throw them away," she said.

"Okay."

"I will."

"So do it," he said.

"You asked for it." She started to walk toward the garbage pail under Charlie's desk, but a little corner of the rug stuck up—it was such a little bit, nobody could possibly notice. But the next thing Maddie knew, she tripped over the rug and fell. When she landed, her legs were sticking up in the air and she held the shoe box high over her head.

"Nice going," Charlie said, and he looked at her in disgust.

"Thank you," Maddie replied—and at that

moment she knew that the one thing she hated almost more than anything in the world was about to happen. It started in the bottom of her stomach, and sure enough, she could feel it moving up to her chest and into her throat. She tried to force it back down, but it was too late. Trying to stop her uncontrollable laughter made her throat ache almost as much as when she had tonsilitis. She couldn't breathe, and so she let out a snort. Charlie looked at her as if she was crazy and turned away.

Maddie laughed. At first the laughs were soft and rhythmic, and she tried to muffle them by covering them with the bottom of her orange sweatshirt; but they quickly became deeper and louder, and then she couldn't stop.

"What's so funny?" Charlie wanted to know.

"You know I can't help it, Charlie," Maddie said, gasping. "I'm not laughing at you."

"Well, it's a stupid habit."

"I know."

"It doesn't make any sense."

"Tell me about it."

"You should go to a doctor or something."

Maddie sat up and looked at him. "For a laugh?" she said, and the thought of it made her laugh even harder. She stared at Charlie, and her eyes were wet and her cheeks were red. She couldn't get any words out; she just sat there shaking her head.

And then something else happened—something

Charlie couldn't have imagined five minutes ago. Not if you'd said that you'd pay him a zillion dollars. The little iceberg in his chest started to melt, and a smile formed at the corners of his mouth—just a tiny one, in case he decided to change his mind. But then he was laughing too, and the laughs got bigger and bigger, and the next thing he knew he pulled a pillow off his bed and bopped Maddie over the head with it, and she was doing the same with another pillow, and Charlie's father actually had to come upstairs and ask them to lower the volume.

When he left, they stared at each other. Finally Charlie walked over to the windowsill and carried a plastic bag to Maddie.

She held out her hands as he tipped it over, and one by one he deposited the missing pieces of the Goodies. Not everything was there, not by a long shot, but she looked down and saw the dog's tail, the father's hat, and part of the mother's arm.

"You fix them," Charlie told her. "You're better at that than me."

"You found them?" she asked.

"It was cinchy," he said.

Maddie stared at Charlie until he had no choice but to look at her. "I'm sorry, Charlie," she said.

He didn't answer, but by the look on his face she knew he knew.

Chapter Thirty-three

That night after dinner—in fact, after everybody else had gone to bed—Charlie and Maddie stood outside in their pajamas and sneakers. There was a soft breeze and a full moon, and they could see the outline of the trees and the gardening sheds and the backs of the houses, all in a row.

"Listen," Charlie said. "It's the peepers."

And sure enough, it was the baby frogs that hatch in the wet banks of the creek every spring.

"Wow! How many of them do you think there are?" Maddie asked. "I'd say at least a billion. Maybe more!"

At first Charlie was about to tell her not to be ridiculous and to explain that a billion is ten times as many as a million, and there could never even be a million. But he looked at her, and instead he said, "You never know."

"Wow."

"I have a secret," he whispered.

"Tell me," Maddie said.

"I'm not afraid of heights."

"I know." She paused. "Charlie, do you think we get more homework in sixth grade?"

"Probably."

"You'll still help me, won't you?"

"Yes."

"And we'll always be friends. Won't we, Charlie?"

"Yes."

"Because deep inside I'm not a mean person, Charlie. You know that, don't you?"

"Yes, Maddie. Yes. Look!"

An owl swooped over their heads and landed deep in the pine tree.

"Hey, Maddie," Charlie whispered.

It was so bright that the light from the moon spilled in between the branches so you could see all the pine needles, one by one, if you wanted to. "I'll race you to the top!"

"Ready when you are," she said. They each placed a foot in front of themselves and an arm behind, like the runners in the Olympics.

Charlie looked at her and grinned. "On your mark, get set, GO!"